In Too Deep

GW01451592

BILLY O'CALLAGHAN

In Too Deep

and other short stories

MERCIER PRESS

IRISH PUBLISHER – IRISH STORY

MERCIER PRESS
Cork
www.mercierpress.ie

Trade enquiries to CMD,
55a Spruce Avenue, Stillorgan Industrial Park,
Blackrock, County Dublin

© Billy O'Callaghan, 2009

ISBN: 978 1 85635 633 6

10 9 8 7 6 5 4 3 2 1

A CIP record for this title is available from the British Library

This book is sold subject to the condition that it shall not, by way of trade or otherwise, be lent, resold, hired out or otherwise circulated without the publisher's prior consent in any form of binding or cover other than that in which it is published and without a similar condition including this condition being imposed on the subsequent purchaser.

No part of this publication may be reproduced or transmitted in any form or by any means, electronic or mechanical, including photocopying, recording or any information or retrieval system, without the prior permission of the publisher in writing.

All characters, locations and events in this book are entirely fictional. Any resemblance to any person, living or dead, which may occur inadvertently is completely unintentional.

Printed and bound in the EU.

Mercier Press receives financial assistance from the Arts Council/An Chomhairle Ealaíon

To my family.

*Writing is a difficult game, and I am grateful beyond
measure for their support.*

In order to live forever, you have to stop time.

Bob Dylan

A Big Mistake

A shepherd reading philosophy,
Immersed in sweet light of a summery day,
Says aloud to his sleepy herd:
My soul should be a singing bird.

The shepherd bought a book on music,
And gave up solitude to join the public.
To him, sadly, knowledge did not belong
– He could not write a beautiful song.

Andrew Godsell (1971–2003)

CONTENTS

LOVE SICK

One morning last July, while wedged into my usual stand-ing place on the train, heading into the city and work, I fell headlong into love. The force of it, an actual physical impact, really did rock me in my shoes, and in that instant I fully understood what people in those old films meant when they talked about the thunderbolt.

The girl was perched on an aisle seat midway back through the carriage, almost as if she had been placed there just for me. The stretch of aisle between us was clogged with people, arms gripping overhead handrails and shoulders that shifted constantly in an effort at balance, but I could see her perfectly. Her hair hung in a straight, almost old-fashioned, shoulder-length style and my mind can still picture even now the way its hazel colour gleamed like rich honey whenever blades of sunlight jabbed past the trees lining the track and through the window. Her interest was fully on the novel that lay open in her lap, so I had time to study her, but the fact of the matter was that a single moment would have been enough, the time left over a luxurious pleasure, but hardly necessary. Perhaps I had formed a false impression, had been sucked into judging a book by its cover, like so many before me, and maybe familiarity and the long, slow passage of time would have worn away the edges until nothing of substance remained. But in that one second, faster than the turn of a coin, I was stricken, truly sickened to my bones with the kind of torment that could only have been love. My throat ached with the effort of breathing; I had never seen anyone quite like her before.

If I had a type, she would have been it, I decided; petite, like a porcelain trinket, all nimble delicacy. She wore a white blouse with the sleeves rolled midway up her slender wrists, and a pair of sky-blue jeans that might have been distantly related to some low-ranking designer, but then again may have simply been a cheap, poorly-cut knockoff. Her legs were crossed demurely at the knee and a scarlet slip-on shoe hung from the toes of her otherwise naked foot. I stared openly, my hunger for details ravenous.

After a few minutes of stalemate, the train jolted, and she was jerked from her story. The book flopped shut in her hands; something by Anne Tyler, though I couldn't make out the title from my inverted vantage point. She gazed around as if just escaping a dream, and then her eyes met mine and it was the turn of her world to change. Her mouth fell agog, honestly, and the colour, what little there had been, seeped from her face. I could see that she was pretty, though not unaccountably so. Certainly, she was a long step out of the league of the world's greatest beauties. But she had the same fresh glimmer as the morning, a youthful vigour that made her as hallowed and insubstantial as dew-tinged air, and that essence was truly captivating.

I found myself pushing through the crowded aisle, muttering apologies along the way whenever I bumped a back or stepped on a blocking foot, but not really caring much about the discomfort I was causing. On a sliding scale of importance, every other passenger on this train was rooted at the bottom, somewhere firmly out of sight. Only this girl mattered.

When I reached her seat I got down on one knee, gently took her hand from where it lay on the book – *The Clock Winder* I now saw – and asked her, right then and there, to marry me. Blushing and just a little panicked, she glanced up at the faces of the other passengers who, curious and amused, were pressing in like new moons, and then she bowed her head and mumbled that, actually, she was already engaged. 'Engaged is not married,' I told her, not really sure where this daring was coming from, because this was completely new territory for me. Usually I struggle to say two words to a stranger, especially a woman. Her hand was still trapped by my fingers, and her flesh was soft and milky, the bones of her inner wrist spindle-thin beneath the skin. I traced the tangle of veins a little way up her arm and decided that I wanted to play that game forever.

At last, she looked up again, and she was smiling. Her eyes were large, at least in staring mode, a two-toned shade of brittle glassy green imbedded in a darker and less tangible base colour, and if her nose was slightly too big and her chin a touch too defined, then it was love's task and duty to re-align such details to fit its own mysterious symmetry. 'Okay,' she said, and her voice seemed to come from the air all around, like a word from heaven, soft and truthful. 'Yes, I'll marry you.'

We got off the train at the next stop. Everything was coming up smiles, and the world seemed to bristle with possibility. We both had other places to be, but work had lost all sense of importance. The big white clock-face in the station proclaimed the time as closing in on nine o'clock and we had the entire day to be together. 'The first day of the rest of our lives,' I whispered against the ridge of her jaw just below her ear. A vague downy fuzz coated her flesh just there, a most delightful discovery. My words, warm with my breath, caused her cheek to tug back in a joyful smile, and I knew in my heart that I would have gone to war for her. Nothing could be allowed to come between us.

The streets were alive with our excitement, a teeming rumble of traffic noise and busy people. We walked aimlessly, holding hands and swapping tangles of nearly delirious conversation, and whenever we grew tired or thirsty we'd stop off at some street-side café to drink coffee and consider each other from different angles and perspectives. She enjoyed cappuccinos, she said, and each small revelation fused embarrassment with pleasure, another step along in the flowering of what really had to be love. I told her that I enjoyed watching her drink them. Her first sip daubed froth onto the tip of her nose, and I leaned in and kissed it away, making her laugh. Our first kiss, I said, and she said that it was nice but that we should try to make our second even better. So we did.

I told her that I could be lazy, sometimes, that actually laziness has marked my life. Honesty was important, I said, and she agreed that it was. 'It's only fair that you know what you are letting yourself in for. The truth is that I'm not really the great prize I might appear to be.' She looked me up and down, cleared her throat in an exaggerated way and nodded yes, but she was smiling. I told her that I'd suffered a kind of breakdown once, when I was seventeen. I'd been accepted into Cambridge to read history, but just prior to my going something seemed to knot up inside of me and after a lot of deliberation I decided that I probably wasn't best suited to an academic career.

Instead I took a job with a delivery company, work that I could do without any thought at all. My father told me in no uncertain terms that I was wasting my life. There was no arguing with the fact that I had a natural and obvious aptitude for packing away the least little filaments of information, no matter how obtuse or archaic, but the simple truth was that history held no appeal for me. Really, I didn't think I knew what I wanted.

'Despite what everyone else thinks, I do believe that not going to Cambridge was all for the best.' She cradled her large cup in the straightened fingertips of both hands, sipped relentlessly through the pale froth for the kick of coffee underneath, and barely nodded. 'You should know right from the beginning,' I said, my tone more than half-serious, 'that I may be the least ambitious person in the entire country. Maybe even in all of Europe. Goals and achievements just don't tickle my happy button. I sometimes like to tell myself that I'm going to write a book one day, but millions of people live a little of this fantasy, and I doubt that I'll ever get around to putting a word of it down on paper. I mean, I don't even have an idea. How is that for a head-start?'

'I don't care about any of that,' she said, after staring into my eyes for half a minute or so. A little smear of chocolate clotted one corner of her mouth, lying on her lip like a sweet bruise, and she fished at it with her tongue, missed and gave up on it. I thought about taking it with a kiss, but decided that maybe I'd be overplaying my hand, forcing things a little too much. It's funny, the things that can cause us regret. Anyway I folded a paper napkin into a tight triangle, reached out with one corner and gently wiped the mark away. 'There must be more to life than work and dusty old books,' she said. 'We're meant to be together, and that's all that counts.'

A second cappuccino was required before she could bring herself to open up, but that, I could see, was merely her nature. I held her hand across the table while she talked, her small shy voice inflecting music into her words, tossing out details of her upbringing and of her own hopes and dreams. There were things I wanted to know, but I let her flit from subject to subject, not wanting to interrupt. We'd have years of time for questions, I told myself, so I feasted on her offerings and understood her a little better with each passing minute.

She loved to sing, she said, and it took no effort of imagination at all for me to imagine her on a stage, perhaps leaning against a piano, basking in the rainy jazz of something husky and sublime. In my mind I could see that she was born for the chalky wash of a spotlight. She adored Sinatra's voice, said that she must have thirty or forty of his albums, and not CDs either, but the old long-players. Over the past couple of years or so, she had developed a sort of hobby out of wandering around the charity shops. Expendable Saturday afternoons put to some use, she said. 'You'd be amazed at the things people give away, nowadays.' The staff in these places were all volunteers, and they had come to know her over time. Her tastes, too. Anything that might be of interest to her, she said, they'd just put to one side, which was how she had managed to gather such a horde of records. An ambition of hers was to wear them down to stumps, to drain every drop of music from them until they had nothing left to give. I smiled with pleasure at her enthusiasm, but when I asked if she would sing for me she looked around, blushed again, and said that she'd like that, but not now. Later, when we could be alone together. Those blushes made me ache for her.

After a while, she grew silent. We were walking, holding hands, and had taken a detour through a park. A few paces in and the trees masked the buildings, a few paces further and the city might not have existed at all. Clouds lay in heavy tufts across the sky, so the late morning seemed to wax and wane, the brightness a genuine effort and the settling gloom a far more natural state, but just then the sun had broken through and the leaves of the manicured alders shuffled to the light beat of a warm breeze. She led me to a bench just off the pathway and we sat. I leaned back and stretched my arm along the latticed rail so that we were just a slip away from an embrace, but she perched stiff and upright and I knew that she was wrestling with some important concern.

Her hand touched my thigh and settled there, her narrow fingers gently splayed, and her mouth pinched up in a serious way, her upper teeth pinching dimples into the soft flesh of her lower lip. Then she spoke.

'When I was seventeen, I became pregnant by a friend of my father's. That sounds worse than it actually was, and we did keep our relationship a secret, but it really wasn't as if he was abusing me or anything. It just sort of happened.' Her eyes fixed into a trance state, staring out along the grassy fringe, and shone wetly with the morning's light, but I could see that this was the only way she could bring herself to broach the subject. Reality had to be blurred. She said that she had thought it was love, because she didn't know any better, but of course she learned the hard way that it wasn't love at all, or anything even close to it. She had the baby aborted, as that was the best thing for everyone. Her father would have gone berserk and her mother's health wasn't all that great. It would have torn their lives apart and it just didn't seem fair to put that stress on them. Besides, she said, she had been just seventeen, with little or no knowledge of the world. A baby would have ruined her life, too. I listened, and read things into her distant gaze and the wavering lilt of her voice. Her father's friend had dealt with everything, making all the necessary arrangements, settling the bills with cash. He collected her at a pre-arranged place, in the car park of their local shopping centre, dropped her off at the clinic and waited in a bar around the corner until she and the doctor had taken care of business. It had been a lot easier than she'd imagined, too; not that terrible at all, really. 'Easier than having a tooth pulled,' she said, bending her mouth up into a smile that nearly fit.

But here was the thing; since then, once a month and just as regular as a new moon, she found herself dreaming of a child. 'In the dreams, everything seems perfectly normal.' The smile clung tenuously to her lips, out of synch with the general stiffness of the rest of her face. A couple of folds creased her forehead, too vague yet to leave any lingering trace, but certainly a start, a sign of what lay ahead. 'At first, I told myself that this was just coincidence, that people drift in and out of dreams all the time, but when the next month came and he was there again, and then again the month after that, I decided that it was probably a natural reaction to what had happened and that in time I'd begin to forget. Except I haven't forgotten. It's been seven years now and there he is, every month, as real as you or me. My little boy. I really do believe that. And he is the most beautiful boy that you could ever hope to see. Every month he's a little further along, growing all the time. I can still remember how it felt to breastfeed him as an infant, and I know his smell and the way he used to grip my finger in his tiny hand. As a baby he had jet-black hair and wide green eyes. The sort of eyes that seem to understand everything. Now when he comes he is tall and slim, with a strong look of his father. I've bathed him, walked him by the hand to his first day of school, held him in my arms while he cried away the pain of a skinned knee. Now I stand and cheer while he wrestles his way through football games. He looks born to run, and I feel so proud when some of the other parents pass some remark on how natural he seems with a ball. Talented, they say, and I smile and try to remain modest, but I know that they can see me glowing.'

What was there to say to that? Air is a peculiar medium in that, sometimes, it can actually conduct pain. When she risked a glance at me and then hurriedly averted her eyes again, I could do nothing else except lean in and kiss her cheek. Her skin masked some inner furnace.

'I've never told anyone about my dreams,' she said. 'Or about the abortion. Even my fiancé doesn't know. But I don't want any secrets between us. It's best that you see the worst of me. I won't blame you if you want to run away.' I laid my hand high on her back, between the poking fins of her shoulder blades, and rubbed as softly as I could. She seemed very frail; the nubs of her backbone could be felt clearly through her skin and the thin cotton of her blouse. The moment lay hard between us, and then, in abject surrender, she turned and just folded her body into my embrace. I could tell that she was crying only by the feel of her breath pulling harshly through her back, and I whispered sounds that were designed to soothe and made the sort of promises that recognised boundaries, that settled for compassion rather than absolution, telling her that it was okay, really, that neither of us were perfect, but that maybe we could be perfect together. Maybe, in time, we could even work out a way for me to be a part of those dreams. 'I love football,' I said, which was true.

I waited until she had boarded the train. It was late evening, not yet dark, but with that belt of dusk that settles on July evenings of a certain vintage and seems to hold its ground for hours. She had business that needed attending, she said, pulling a tired expression. The business of breaking a heart. Her fiancé would be upset, of course, but he'd cope. She didn't want to hurt him, but what they had together was comfort rather than joy, fun but without the fireworks. Maybe he'd even feel some relief, she said, but the words were wishful rather than certain. After all, they'd been engaged seven months, and they'd still not gotten around to fixing a date yet. She hoped that he wouldn't hate her for what she was doing, but if he did then she'd just have to find a way of dealing with that. I watched her while she scribbled down her telephone number on a piece of scrap paper, and I took the number, read it once, then folded it into my wallet. There was plenty of room in there, she remarked, and we both laughed at that. Then the train came, and we stood at the carriage's door for as long as we could, kissing, holding hands and making promises about the things we'd do that night, and tomorrow, and in all the years to come.

Ten minutes later my own train rattled into view, and I boarded with the few others who were waiting, found a mostly empty carriage near the back and sank down into a double seat. I didn't want to think about how it would be for her as she arrived at her fiancé's door, but the image of that scene wouldn't let me be, so finally I just gave up and basked in it, seeing the apartment or house door open and his smiling, surprised expression at finding her there. Maybe an outstretched arm taking his weight against the door's jam. I winced as I imagined him leaning in to kiss her hello, and wondered if she would let him do that or if she would turn her face away in a gesture that told him everything even before the brutal glut of words had loosed themselves in her throat. There was no telling how he would take the news, though devastation seemed a likely enough reaction. And at least half of that was my fault, probably even more than half. After all, I had made the running, I had waded uninvited in to someone else's life. I tried to watch the flashes of passing, dusk-laden landscape streaking past the window, the city's boroughs thinning so gradually out to grand swathes of countryside and then filling up once more into the next pocket of town, but the world seemed different, smaller somehow, and more washed-out. My mind was in a state of turmoil, and refused to focus. Little unrelated details of the day kept flailing at me, snagging like barbed hooks and then tearing painfully away.

Maybe this was part of the reason why I failed to sense the danger. My apartment was across town from the station, close to a mile of walking. There were taxis waiting around in the little yard behind the platform, but the sky held a few small cracks of light yet and I was probably thinking that the walk would do me some good. I had just entered a side street when two men closed in. I'm not sure how I had failed to notice them but it took less than a second to survey my situation and recognise it as dire. A knife flashed, the sort of blade that threatens the wise and plunders the stupid. One of the men had gotten behind me somehow and there was nowhere to run, nothing to do, but give them what I had and hope they'd have the sense not to go spilling blood.

After they had run away I leaned against the wall. The bricks were cold and damp, despite the time of year, with a thin, greasy sheen of mould. They had taken all my money, over a hundred pounds, but more than that, they had taken my wallet, too. The cards could be cancelled, and that was an irritant but a relatively straightforward process, a well-enough trodden path, I suppose, given the kind of world we live in today. And the wallet, of course, could be replaced, even if it did have the sentimental value of being the very same piece of leather that my father had given to me on my eighteenth birthday, packing into its folds a wisp of straw from that year's nativity crib. Good luck, he said that was. He had put a lot of effort into straightening out the wrinkles of his accent, but his Irish blood still bubbled to the surface on occasion, superstition and sentimentality being the main triggers. I suppose my birthday had called for both barrels. 'Keep the straw tucked away there and your wallet might never be overflowing, but it will never be empty, either.' He had been right about that, the way he was right about a lot of things that never made sense to me, though there had been plenty of days since when that piece of straw must have found it pretty lonely going, trapped inside that sweaty leather with nothing but pennies for company.

The only thing of real value had also been taken, the scrap of paper with the inky scribble of her telephone number, the most precious thing in my entire world. The wallet was out of my hand before I had even realised what I was losing. I tried to call after my muggers, wanting to tell them that they could take the money and the cards if they wanted but to please, for Christ's sake, just give me back the piece of paper. It could have meant nothing to them. But they were already running and probably thought that I was simply calling for help. Or maybe they just didn't care one way or the other. I remember nothing at all about them apart from the staring, heroin-fevered eyes of the one who waved the blade, the sort of eyes that could never be moved to mercy, not once the hunger for a fix had taken over. I don't need anyone to tell me that I should be down on my knees giving thanks to God for the fact that they chose to leave me with my life, as insignificant a thing to them as the withered piece of straw that they'd find book-marking the tens and twenties.

But I don't feel like being grateful, because I can't believe that God had much of a hand in what happened. I mean, what kind of God would tease a man with a glimpse of heaven and then kick him tumbling and screaming back down again into the depths of a despairing hell? Those who hold with religious beliefs like to explain misery away by saying that we all have our crosses to bear, but I find it difficult to accept that, at twenty-five years old, the peak of my life was to be represented by something as seemingly inconsequential as a scribbled number on a scrap of paper.

That was eleven months ago. I've passed the time since doing what anyone in my position would have done: I rode the train every morning and evening, and lay awake nights dredging my memories for some tiny, vital snippet of information that I may have overlooked. But, so far, it's all been to no avail. I can picture her exactly in my mind, down to the most minute of details, and I have even made a considerable job of recreating the subjects of our rambling discussions. We talked about everything, and yet we talked about nothing at all. It was a shock to realise that she had made no mention of her address, or where she worked. She had never even offered me her surname. These revelations, when stated in such bald terms, seem to make light of my claims that what had flashed between us was anything as deep as love, but we are talking about mere words, not rushing pulses and chasing hearts. Love is like trying to create fire or water from thin air, the very same sort of magic.

I can't bear to imagine the terrible things that must be running through her mind; that perhaps I suffered an accident or, worse still, that I changed my mind. I suppose she must think that I've run away because of what she told me, but the truth is that actually I love her all the more for that. Not for doing what she did, of course, but for her willingness to confide in me, to make me feel that there was nothing we couldn't tell one another, no matter how terrible. It is difficult to live with the knowledge that, even though I didn't mean to, I have hurt her by not being in contact, but if I think too much about such things I'll never have enough strength to keep searching.

My life is focused on finding her. I ride the train every morning and every evening, and at weekends I traipse around the charity shops that are scattered across the city, telling my story to the volunteer workers, any who will listen. Some have mentioned that they think they know who I mean, a girl, yes, who likes records, dark-haired and thin, though my intense descriptions don't spark much of a response in their eyes. I leave them my name, address and phone number, and they take pity on me and say that, okay, if someone wanders in professing an interest in Sinatra records they will pass the message along. I want more than that, but I thank them for the little they give. So far, I've had no luck.

Possibly the most galling thing is the fact that I actually read the phone number before folding it away in my wallet for safekeeping. I've tried everything short of hypnosis to bring it back to the surface of my mind, but the few times that I thought I had it the phone rang out or the number I dialled wasn't valid. Hypnosis is an option, I suppose, if a bit of a last resort.

She remains stubbornly real in my mind, and yet I can't help but feel a whisper of doubt. Ghosts are real, too, and dreams, but real in different ways. My lowest ebb comes when, overwhelmed by loneliness and desperation, I reach for the telephone book and call up the first person I find that matches her name, and while listening to the line buzzing with the anticipation of my call I squeeze my eyes shut, because miracles feel more conducive to such a darkness. I've succumbed to this a hundred times, two hundred, trusting to fate that on one of these occasions the voice that answers will be hers. But doubt has grounded itself in the fact that, after almost an entire year of searching, I have yet to find a single trace of her existence.

All my hopes are pinned now on next month. The day is circled on my calendar, and I've planned exactly how I will recreate that first meeting. Our anniversary. I'll stand in the same carriage on the train, the very spot if I can find it, and I will get off at an early stop and wander the streets, sit and drink coffee, maybe even cappuccino. Finally, I'll sit on our bench in the park. I keep telling myself that she'll be there too, somewhere along the way, looking for me. The world is just too small a place for something as big as love to be kept apart for long. While there's life, there's hope.

SECRETS

It was late in the afternoon when he entered the café. He paused in the doorway and waited for his eyes to adjust themselves to the gloom, then he raised a hand to the waitress, turned and went back outside. After a minute or so, the waitress followed him out. She was tall and young, very pretty, with her dark hair pulled back in a way that fully accentuated the sharpness of her cheekbones and the rich green of her eyes. She considered him as he sat before her and quickly dismissed his chances, and after that she became distracted. He looked up at her as he ordered, waving away the offer of a menu and settling instead for a glass of the house red, but she had seen all she wanted to see and refused to meet his eyes. She just scrawled down his order on a small notepad, nodded and sauntered back inside.

Well, he decided, as he watched her retreat, maybe she wasn't all that beautiful. She had a little upturn to her nose, a quirk that probably had all the boys swooning now, while her flesh was still young, but which would turn ugly in a hurry once the wrinkles set in.

He was glad of his overcoat. He put his hands in his pockets and sank down inside the collar. This was not the weather for sitting outside. It was dry, for now, but the air was sharpened by a cold breeze that swept in waves down along the river and, overhead, the restless sky moiled layer upon layer, muddy spools ghosting beneath a steely veneer. There would be snow by morning, maybe even by nightfall. The few other patrons had all elected to accept the sanctuary of the café, but he preferred it out here, despite the cold. All the keenness of the morning had faded, giving ground to a kind of stupor. The imminent closing in of evening would bring with it a second wind, that tumbling darkness so rich with whispered promise, with murmurs of love, adventure and the thrill of the hunt, but for him none of those things could compete with the empty yawn that so defined Montmartre during late afternoon. He found this stretch of day to be most soothing, comfortable in its own lack of expectation; contentment, he had learned, lay in the still moments.

When his wine came he didn't bother to look at the waitress, or even to speak. He was finished with all of that now. She set the glass down on a folded paper napkin, muttered something that he didn't quite catch, probably some exhortation to enjoy, and then she was gone again, in a hurry to be inside. He sat, legs crossed, and turned the glass with slow care, around and around. The table's yellow-flecked formica surface squealed resistance, stopping only when he helped himself to a sip. Good or bad was all the same to him, wine was wine and he'd never honed his palate to any level of expertise. All he knew was that its taste suited him, and that if he put away a sufficient quantity of the stuff he'd get to where he needed to be.

A woman was watching him. He noticed her almost as soon as he had sat down; she took up one edge of a bench just across the street, her frail posture nervous nearly to the point of apology as she hunched over a ragged paperback novel. While he waited for his wine to arrive he had surveyed the street; his eyes had noticed her and then passed her by. Now, when he looked again, in the same casual manner as before, he was startled to find that she was watching him. Her novel was still in place, wedged open in her lap with the encouragement of a book-marking thumb, but, for now anyway, it was forgotten. For a moment, he began to question whether or not she was watching him, wondered if perhaps she had simply fallen into a trance that just happened to lie somewhere off in his direction, but when he raised a hand in greeting, the friendliest gesture he could think to make, she stirred and looked hurriedly away, and the panicked sharpness of her reaction removed all doubt. From all the way across the street he could feel her embarrassment. A few minutes passed, but just when it was beginning to seem that she had finished with him, there it was, another quick, daring turn of the head, another risked glance, and this time he was ready for her. He rose a little from his chair and beckoned to her. She seemed to stiffen, probably trying to decide whether to acknowledge him or to run away. Then, abruptly, she flopped her book shut and stood.

She had a lithe way of moving, a dancing walk that was all toe and hardly any heel, and she flitted across the road, judging the flush of the traffic and stuttering from lane to lane. As she drew closer, certain details began to emerge. He saw that she was young, a little older than the waitress perhaps, but still a distance shy of her thirties. She was small and frail, with narrow shoulders, thin limbs and a pale oval face made haggard by inner things. He stood when she drew to within a few yards and tried to smile away her uncertainty. 'Please,' he said, making his voice as soft as it would go, 'won't you join me?' She paused and glanced around, looking either for an excuse or a reason to escape, then lowered her eyes in small surrender. Feeling his heart beating more quickly than it had in a long time, he pulled out a chair for her, the gentlemanly thing to do, and she sat, perching almost weightlessly on its edge.

Now that they were close, there seemed less to say. He studied her, carving her details into his mind; the anxious pull of her thin lips, the nose that seemed too wide for her face, its hammered-down bridge broken almost to perfect flatness with her cheeks, the tiny furrows that grooved the paper-thin skin of her high forehead. Her hair had been badly cut, falling to shoulder-length in uneven ropes the colour of washed-out sand and leaning thickly out from the sides of her head, and her clothes were cheap and possibly second-hand, all coarse wools and ill-matched flannels. Unkempt was the word that described her best. If there was beauty in evidence then it had to be largely imagined, yet for all of that he knew in his heart that it was there.

They ordered more wine and filled the silences with sips and tiny blushing smiles. There were things that he thought of asking, but didn't, because whatever it was that they had found between them was finely balanced and a wrong word now could very well tip everything out of synch. He decided to let her take all the risks and confined himself to straight answers and insignificant small talk.

She too was hesitant with words. She held her glass in spindle-thin fingers and spoke in a small, cracked voice into its rim. When the words came, asking him about what it was that he did, where he lived, where he was from originally, the airy effort of them flared her broad nostrils and caused her upper lip to sink a little. On anyone else in the world that detail would have weighed as resolutely ugly, but on her it didn't seem that way at all. In fact, after ten minutes of stilted conversation, he felt something shift inside of him and he knew that he would long forevermore to hear that voice. She had come to Paris from the south, she said, waving away the need to mention exactly where. Paris wasn't all she'd hoped it would be, but it wasn't so bad either. She worked mornings in one of the bigger used-book-shops along the West Bank, had a small bed-sit that she could just about afford, and liked to fill her after-work hours with walks through the city. 'There are some perks to the job,' she said, raising the novel that she'd been gripping the entire time. The corners of her mouth curled when she said that, and he nodded and smiled too, though he detected a sadness in her that he wanted more than anything to just kiss away. The novel's cover was pale yellow and blank now that the embossed words had worn to nothing. He decided that with a closer look he could probably have made out the title, or at least the author, but suddenly it seemed better not to know.

Somehow, an hour passed. The evening had taken on the bruised tinge of dusk and without even realising, they had drawn closer together. He cleared his throat, suddenly realising that her face lay mere inches from his own; so close, in fact, that he believed he could feel the press of her breath against his cheek.

'It's getting late,' she whispered, and she glanced up at the sky and shuddered. Grasping the opportunity, he reached out and laid his hand on hers, closing his fingers gently over the backs of her knuckles. Her flesh felt very cold, and he wondered if she would feel this way all over.

'Can I walk you home?' he asked, and she hesitated, drained the last of the wine from her glass, then nodded.

'I'd like that very much,' she said.

They walked through the evening streets, she linking his arm, their bodies drawn together against the chill of the late hour. Walking, and perhaps being spared the need to meet her eye, he felt more inclined toward talk than he had all day. Words welled up inside of him and spooled from his mouth in curls of fog, gossamer-hued and delicate. His voice felt choked down to a murmur, but set strangely free; he spoke of things he had never told anyone. Not quite outright, because he wasn't yet ready for that, but enough to suggest the hidden truths of his life. Mostly about the war and how difficult it had been for him, how he had prayed to find some sort of understanding in the whole sorry mess, pleading with God to grant him the strength to carry the weight of all that he had seen and done. As he spoke, he watched the traffic drift by, considered the dark corners and alleyways, and all the shuttered windows that caged in so many other lives. Beside him, he felt his companion tighten her grip and occasionally nod her head in answer to the ebb and flow of his confessions, silently urging him on, wanting to know him inside as well as out. This woman who, just hours ago, had been a stranger, now felt like the person he knew best in the entire world. The stories they swapped were merely background colour; what they had discovered in one another ran to great depths. It was not the exposing of secrets that mattered so much, because the true mercy was in the listening. He talked of the war, not needing to describe the carnage because some things were understood, and then, with even greater care, ventured on to other things.

When they reached her building, she broke gently from him, found her keys and opened the door. He stood in the cobbled street, patiently considering the silent, crumbling façades of the neighbouring buildings, the splintered plaster, the exposed grey and yellow stonework, the faded flaking paint on the doors and window frames. He waited until she stepped into the dimly lit hallway, then obeyed the silent invitation and followed her up the three flights of stairs, climbing slowly to keep pace with her and talking all the way, unable to stop now, as if the silence waiting to fall might ache with too harsh a judgement. Somewhere deep inside of him a dam had broken and the muscles of his throat twitched in spasms against the lurching torrents. From the war, he drifted on to other things, following an order often without reason, the subjects suddenly rearing their heads and just as suddenly dissipating.

She opened the door of her apartment and led him inside, urging him to sit while she made a pot of coffee.

The apartment was small and sparsely decorated. Without wanting to be seen to stare, he registered a bed, a worn-out armchair and a little kitchenette consisting of stove, sink, fridge and a single cupboard. One wall was bare brick, powdery yellow, the sort of thing that would have been distinctly fashionable if done intentionally, but all the others were decked out in a pale-coloured paper that had given up its pattern probably generations ago. Paperback novels piled up in leaning stacks from the floor just beneath the window, the obvious explanation for the damp, mouldy smell that weighed down and choked the air. While his mouth rambled on, he stared transfixed at the gaudy covers of the books, noting the rearing horses of throwaway westerns and the butch, bare-chested men and scantily clad damsels in distress of serial romances. Across the room, she filled the kettle and set the water to boil, but continued to listen to what he had to say, nodding her head in all the right places, urging him on with little humming sounds whenever he began to wane.

The coffee seemed to staunch the flow of his words. She sat beside him and they sipped in silence. The coffee was a precursor, cleaving the next couple of hours' schedule in stone, and neither of them felt quite sure how to act or what else to say. They sipped, rabid for the heat and nervous about what would follow. Finally, she set down her cup and, without saying anything, stood, turned ever so slightly away into profile and began to undress. He watched her until she was more or less halfway through, a part of him wanting to smile at the determination that pinched her face, the rest of him wanting to sweep her up in his arms. Once she was naked to the waist, it began to feel almost unseemly to stare. Trembling inside, he pulled off his tie and slowly undid the buttons of his shirt.

When he was naked, she took his hand and led him to the bed. The sheets felt cold, and for a while they fumbled with one another, all gasping breath and uncertain grunts. She seemed almost too delicate to touch. Lying there on the bed, her wide pale eyes surveying everything, she could have been a child. Her body was rail thin, disturbing in its seeming fragility, ribs and hip bones jutting up through the vague film of her skin. With a feather touch, he let his hands caress the scant breasts that lay splayed flat against her chest, his fingers plucking at the small, hard, unripened berries of her nipples.

'I know you,' she whispered, as he kissed her. 'I know who you are.' Her hands stroked his shoulder blades and traced the ripples of his spine down into the small of his back, and her hips pushed at him, calling for some response. But there was some obstacle in the way, some blockage in his mind. He kissed her cheek, trying to buy time or maybe to apologise, then pressed his face down into the pocket of her neck so that he could hide his tears. Feeling the heat of those tears against her skin, she raised her chin, making the fit a snug one. Blood pumped in her veins; he listened to its rush against his ear and tried to imagine the heaving of oceans.

'Don't worry,' she sighed, comfortable beneath his weight. 'It happens. But the world goes on spinning, and there's always time to try again.'

'What did you mean?' he asked, after some time had

passed. He had given up, and now lay huddled beneath the flimsy blanket. The wool smelled of her, the sweat of her skin, but of deeper and even more distinctive scents too, and he drew its edge up to his chin so that he might better savour such an unexpected detail.

She lay beside him, on the brink of sleep, though her hand raked back and forth beneath the blanket, her fingertips teasing and getting to know the down of hair that smattered his chest and stomach.

'When you said you knew me, what did you mean?'

She opened her eyes. Her face lay just inches from his own, and he was again shocked to find a beauty that added up to far more than the mere sum of its flawed parts. 'Just that,' she said, her voice all smoke again, a stunning aural texture. 'I know you.'

'How?' He rolled onto his back, and took to studying the ceiling. He realised that he was afraid of what the answer might be.

'Why, you're me, of course,' she said, with a little hiccup of laughter, as if the answer were obvious. 'I mean, we're the same, you and I. Looking at you is like looking in a mirror. We carry around the same sort of secret, but there are others like us, too many others. I can always tell them at a glance. Anyone can, if they know how to read the signs. Some are more clearly marked than others. With certain people the evidence might not be much, just a hardness around the mouth, a distance to their stare, the way they hold their shoulders when they walk or how they react to a question asked, but whatever it is, it's still there, and it's enough. Today, as soon as I saw you, I knew.'

'From all the way across the street. Am I that obvious?'

'Let's put it this way: you're not difficult to read.'

She pressed her mouth against the lobe of his ear and kissed the falling line of his jaw. When she smiled, sadly, he could feel it seeping into the bones of his skull. 'What was it for you? An orphanage, a neighbour, a teacher at school? An uncle?'

He made a sound with his throat and scraped it clear, but he could still hear it in his mind. 'One of those, all of those,' he said, and then she had reached his lips and he closed his eyes and let her in, surrendering to her, the first person in a long, long time that he really wanted to grant some access to his life, the first who seemed to understand what he was all about.

'If you are serious about surviving, you can't allow the details to matter,' she said. With his eyes closed he could imagine colours in that voice, tangled brown and grey ribbons of smoke or muddy, burnt-out rainbows, and he shifted and reawakened, trying desperately not to fall in love, not yet ready for something as drastic and over-whelming as that.

Without noticing, the hour had grown late, verging close to midnight, and a lamp was burning across the room. 'Do you always sleep with the light on?' he asked.

He felt her nod her head. 'Don't you?'

Rather than answer, he let it go. He watched her fingers worry the fringe of the blanket, and felt his heart break more than a little at the sight of her badly chewed fingernails. A moment earlier, he had been planning the easiest possible manner of escape, working up the excuse that would allow him to just slip away. Now, it seemed easier and better to stay. The tiniest details made all the difference. She propped herself up on one elbow, peeled a rope of fringe back off her face and tucked it behind her right ear. It held its forced position for just a beat, then tumbled back down across her eyes again. He reached out and ran a hand from her armpit slowly down to the jagged peak of her hip, and then she was looming above him again, her mouth smiling, answering some perceived invitation, with every shift of her china doll's body asking the sort of questions that didn't need words. He met her smile and returned it, and though their second attempt was nowhere near a triumph, it was at least a little more successful than the first had been. What was more, it felt like they had sealed some important deal.

THE COST OF LIVING

'I don't look at it that way, Mrs Malone,' I said, helping myself to another sip of Scotch. The living room was expensively decorated, a classy joint from start to finish. The stuff on show was enough to hurt my eyes, but at least it provided a distraction. Too much looking at a girl like Susan Malone could play havoc with a man's best intentions.

'Murder is such an ugly word. I prefer to think of it as business. I'm a problem-solver. People come to me with a problem and I try to help out, if I'm in a position to do so and if the monetary compensation strikes me as acceptable. But I'm not in this business to get caught. I don't gamble, I only play the safe odds.'

God, she was something. You know the type: early thirties, tall and slim, but not skin and bone, with eyes the subtle blue of smoke and long blonde hair bouncing in curls around her bare shoulders. She wore a tasty black satin number, discreetly cut to emphasise her shape. I didn't want to stare, but I guess she was resigned to men staring by then.

'All right,' she said. 'So, what about my problem? Can you help?'

I shrugged. 'Yeah, I guess I can do something for you.' I hadn't noticed before, but she was nervous. Some people move around when they are nervous, others just freeze. I had her down as the cold type.

The details weren't too complicated, nothing I hadn't heard a dozen times before. Basically, she just wanted her husband out of the picture. She had gotten my number from a friend of a friend, and that's usually how it works. Most of my work is corporate-sponsored, and I try to steer clear of domestic jobs, but occasionally I'll make an exception, when the money is too good to refuse.

Jake Malone had money to burn. Officially, he had made his fortune in transport, but most people knew that there was mud beneath the surface, whispers of drugs and Mob affiliations. These days he was clean right down to his toes and, as a respected pillar of the community, involved in all kinds of charity work and a voice of note in the Republican party. He had also expanded his empire to magnate pro-portions. The picture I held in my hand showed a man in his late sixties, bloated by the excesses of living. Not exactly the Prince Charming that every schoolgirl dreams of marrying.

But high finance could be a powerful aphrodisiac. Susan Malone wore her wealth well, yet there was something there that told me she hadn't always been accustomed to such surroundings. Not that I held any of it against her. Quite the contrary, in fact. She used what she had, made the best of it.

We talked money. I named a figure and she shrugged absently, as if it were nothing. I insisted on cash, half up front, and told her not to expect a receipt. Keep the paperwork for the pen pushers.

'Half,' she said, and held out a large brown envelope. 'Count it if you like.' The distance in her voice fit perfectly with the rest of the picture.

'That's all right,' I said, smiling, 'I can trust you, I'm sure.' My reputation was beyond reproach; few would have been foolish enough to try anything as cheap as short-changing me. I never needed to count the cash, and I had never once, in all the years that I have been doing this work, encountered a single problem in collecting the balance.

'When will you … go to work?' she asked, choosing her words carefully. A lot of people are like that. She stood close enough for me to breathe the delicate lily-of-the-valley scent of her perfumed skin, but I had a rule: no mixing business with pleasure. There'd be time for such things later; maybe we could even come to some arrangement in lieu of the balance.

'It's best that you don't know,' I said. 'There's a lot more involved than just pulling the plug. It could be weeks, maybe even a couple of months. You won't hear from me for a while, even after it's all over. But I'll call when the time is right.'

She nodded, and that was that.

The people who tend to find themselves on my list are invariably the sort best put out to dry. The Mob pays most of my bills; gangsters keep themselves generally well protected, but I can build a plan to fit any situation. Sometimes, I can do my work from a mile away, peering through a sniper's scope and just cutting loose, but even if I'm being paid to send an added message and I have to get my hands dirty, I rarely have to break a sweat. The police will take a look, but they won't go digging, because Mob hits are part of the daily merry-go-round.

Domestic jobs are more difficult, because of the level of trust that I have to extend, a concept quite foreign to my nature. In an 'accident', the grieving spouse is naturally first in the firing line. Most people think they can handle the heat, but they'll start spilling at the first upward click of the thermostat. And this is where attention to detail comes in. It is imperative that the police don't query the death as anything other than accidental. Hence my hefty price-tag.

Jake Malone was six foot of bloated girth, with the thunderous ego that men who measure their wealth in the hundreds of millions wear like a sidearm. Sixties isn't ancient, but on a man like him it was plenty. Susan was his trophy wife, and I found myself hoping for her sake that it never strayed much further than the ornamental state. When I am casing a job, I do my utmost to remain detached from such useless emotions as like or dislike, but there was no denying that this guy was a hunting accident waiting to happen.

'I'll leave that up to you,' Susan had said, when I mentioned some possible methods. 'I have it on good authority that you are considered the very best in your field, so I guess I'd be a fool not to let you take care of the details. Besides, it's not as if I hate him or anything like that.' I weighed her words for the least hint of flirtation, and nodded.

So there it was; just business. A lady who knew what she wanted out of life and was not afraid to go after it. I wondered if she could ever fall for someone like me. I'm in good shape and not bad-looking for mid-forties, and I've managed to put aside a nice little nest-egg to ensure a very comfortable retirement. Some women even found ambrosial qualities in my aura of menace. I decided that, when all of this was done, I'd come knocking.

I took my time with the job, gave the situation a chance to settle. A cooling period is important, in case of new developments or stirrings of conscience. And when, finally, I did set to work, Jake Malone was still brash and overweight, still rolling to his routine days, making the office by ten, lunching with a constantly rotating clientele, and always checking out by five. I kept up surveillance for a fortnight, until I could read him like a penny dreadful.

Like a lot of his kind, he liked the façade of independence, and found great appeal in the idea of showing the world that he had never lost touch with the common man. No personal valets for him, no chauffeurs either. When he left work at five, he climbed behind the wheel of a jet-black Lincoln Navigator SUV, a great boat-like slab that practically haemorrhaged cash, but which held a lot of sway as a style statement among the tasteless glitterati. Such indulgence made him an easy mark though, allowing me to trail him at a variety of distances and to watch how he bullied his way through rush-hour traffic, cutting lanes, running red lights and blasting his horn at anyone who dared hold their place instead of ceding right of way to him. The man was a maniac behind the wheel and that presented me with an open-door invitation. All I had to do was find a quiet spot on the road and go to work. The police would open and shut the books on this highway wreck, no question about it.

Malone always took the hill route home. The hill, seven or eight miles out of town, was the status real estate, and his spread was the prime spot: well elevated, west-facing for bloody sunsets and the sparks of the town lighting up as stars in the darkness. The road up was narrow and winding, and edged in several places on sheer drops. It wouldn't take much to ease him out into the waiting abyss.

The whole thing looked straightforward, but as always, my mind was soaked in doubt. What if I had underestimated his abilities as a driver? What if he saw me coming in my freshly stolen sedan and merely sneered as he held his place, and his cool? Or maybe I'd have the bad luck of meeting oncoming traffic just as I made the final push. And all would be lost. But some risks were unavoidable, and I have always been good at working out mathematical equations, measuring the angles, settling on the correct formula. Besides, doubt is, I think, an essential part of my work.

In the end, the job proved as easy as picking flowers.

He had the needle pinned in the high seventies and it was all the sedan could do, given the steepness of the incline, to close the gap. Still, the speed was the key; the faster he was going the easier it would be for me to make him to lose control. When I made my move, edging up beside him, I registered anger in his eyes. Then I swerved, hard but still keeping control, but his reflexes were slow and to avoid being hit he pulled hard at the wheel, all that anger engulfed by terror. A heartbeat later, I was past and the SUV had torn through the whitewashed guard-rail.

I slowed, because breaking too suddenly could have left marks on the asphalt, and the next bend revealed to me the twisted metal of the wreckage, far below. Then, seconds later, the gas tank ignited and an explosion ripped apart the day. Knowing that my work was done, I didn't stop.

I usually wait a year before getting back in touch with a client, but this time I had other things in mind than money. The woman I had widowed was bearing up very well.

'Don't go crying into people's faces,' I had told her. 'It won't look genuine, especially with the age-gap. A better act would be to retreat into yourself, grow thoughtful, distant. And don't rush things. Try to resist the need for … company.'

Clever girl, I thought, the few times I helped myself to a discreet look-in.

Six months to the day, I put in a call. 'You know who this is?' I asked and, after a breathy pause, she said she did. I told her to expect me the following evening at eight, then hung up. Eight was a civilised hour, suggestive without being too brazen.

The inquest had put the cause of death as accidental, with not even a suggestion of anything untoward. By now the estate had been settled and the massive life insurance policy honoured. The cash owed to me was small change in comparison, but I've dealt before with people new to money and I wasn't averse to a spot of bargaining. After all, six months was a long time and women get lonely, just the same as men.

She answered the doorbell wearing jeans and a skimpy white camisole, a beige cashmere cardigan her only effort at modesty. Her hair was pulled back into a casual ponytail and looking darker for the effort, but the style suited her, emphasising the fine bone structure of her face.

'Good evening,' I said and held out the small bunch of flowers, nothing fancy. She took them, letting her movement be thanks enough. Over coffee we swapped a little small-talk; she leaned forward so that she was perched on the edge of an armchair and I helped myself to details. Her left heel had lifted from her slip-on shoe, and even the curve of her arch was enough to set my heart racing.

'I guess you're here for your money,' she said, finally. I sensed a problem in her tone and, I'll admit, it excited me. She steeled herself. Her chin had an eggshell delicacy in the subtle lamplight. 'Actually, I don't think that I'll pay.'

I merely levelled her with a cool stare.

'I've made some enquiries,' she said, 'and the price you originally quoted seems quite exorbitant. Especially since I have only your word that what happened was actually due to your interference.'

I smiled. 'Well, that's the trick. If I had made it any less convincing, we could very well find ourselves waiting in line for the lethal injection.'

'Still,' she said, 'I believe the figure you're asking is more than double your usual fee. I don't like being played for a fool.'

'The figure was high, I'll grant you,' I said, patiently. 'But it was an exceptional situation. At no point did I ever try to play you for a fool. On the contrary, I think I've been very straight with you. You agreed to my demands. Of course, we didn't put anything in writing. I suppose it's only natural to look for a loophole, though most people understand that it's in their best interests to pay up.'

She looked small and tense, but still managed a thin smile.

'Is that a threat?'

I shook my head, no. 'I don't waste my time with threats,' I said. 'What would be the point in mentioning that I know a lot of unsavoury people who are good at making accidents happen, or that I have friends in the police who could, with a little prompting, open up old wounds and make things decidedly difficult for you?'

'You won't do that,' she said. 'That would be putting your own head in the noose.'

'Well, since you bring that up, I have an alibi, a congressman in fact, who will swear up and down a Bible that I was with him that evening. Besides, there's nothing to link me with anything improper.'

She looked close to tears.

'Look,' I sighed, 'like I said, I'm not threatening you. I did what you hired me to do. Maybe I could force you to pay me, but I'm not going to do that.' I stood, pulled on my coat and showed myself to the door. 'Good-bye, Mrs Malone,' I said, 'and good luck.'

That was two years ago. In my entire career, she was the only client who ever stiffed me on a bill. I guess people know about it, people who count, and they probably think that I got my money some other way, or that I'm just a sucker for a pretty face and a nice pair of legs. Maybe they're right.

I never heard from her again. It always felt like the only job that I had left unfinished, and it was unfinished, until this morning.

Suicide, the papers said. As wealthy as she was, her death was high profile enough to make the national rags. The details were sketchy but, apparently, she cut her wrists. I could picture that, her gentle hands, the marble glow of her skin and the incision. Her in the bathtub, naked in a few inches of warm water, her cheeks wet from tears, working up the courage with a bottle of ten-year-old malt whiskey while the straight razor lay in its crooked fold on the tub's porcelain edge. The papers put it down to depression caused by the tragic death of her husband, the transport magnate, Jake Malone, two years earlier. Things like that make nice news, tragic love, a strange kind of happy ending.

Not the way I wanted it, even though she was the one blot on my copybook. Obviously, she took her life because she could no longer live with what she had done. But if she didn't believe after all that her husband's death had been accidental, then really, she should have paid me what I was owed, don't you think?

DOG DAYS

Dog days. That was what Melissa always called them, those January and February Sundays in any midwestern city, when they were down to the stitching of their pockets and the hunger for whiskey had made a festering pit of their bellies. The sort of days when the air has its own sound, when the streets are empty of people yet full of people's waste. Rags of newspaper bound and tumble along, then mildew to death in the sodden gutters, their warnings and promises melting into the same inky pulp, to be forgotten by the world. Melissa is three years gone from Johnny's life, but the dog days still come.

This isn't any kind of town for the likes of you, she used to say. Not for the likes of you.

And actually, there was something in that, some meaning that he glimpsed from time to time but could never quite catch. He listened, almost understanding, but all he could do to ease her pain was nod his head in agreement. She smiled at his lie and so did he, and they both had something to share, even as little as that. He listened to her, but he could not leave, even after he had offered up every promise in the book that, okay, he would, just as soon as he ... because all of that was just whiskey talk and everyone knows that there is no holding to those sort of promises. He told her what she wanted to hear but, as with all his other lies, these were just words spoken to fill the hollows and to add a little variation to the constant strumming of the wind. If she could take some additional solace from what he was saying, if she could somehow persuade herself that she really had reached out and maybe helped save a life, then that was great, so much the better. All he wanted was for her to be happy. But deep down, they both knew that he wouldn't go.

Staying was partly down to the fact that this was a place he knew better than anywhere else in the country, but it had even more to do with the fact that she was there, Melissa, light of his one thing, fire of his other. She was not perfect, of course, but who in the world was, and when she smiled all the bothers slipped away, all the ragged clothes and the dirty hair, all the bad thoughts that nibbled with such fever at her mind. When she smiled she was as pretty as a country morning and that is a memory far more precious than gold. He stayed because of her, and even though she has been gone a long time now, three years, he continues to stay. The reasons for his staying have shifted somewhat, but they have not diminished. The lights may have dimmed, but that is all.

Life out here on the street is defined by the empty stretches, the torpid meandering of darkness into day and then slowly back again. That emptiness breaks a body down, ravages a quick mind down to the slowest liveable beat, but it serves to brilliantly heighten the moments of brilliance and dream, the punctuations of terrible night-time violence and the occasional offered smile. Johnny walks the streets and collects smiles, gathers them up and stores them in his many pockets and in the folds of his clothes, sporting them like badges. Sometimes he is convinced that, worn in such a way, the smiles will protect him from the worst that the dog days have to bring, though they didn't help at all on the morning that Melissa was found. Terrible things happen in every city. When so many people are caged together and armed to the teeth with money and fear, the odds are good that someone in the crowd will be stewing bad thoughts. But even knowing that, even braced against it, it hurts like hell's pitchfork when it stabs your life asunder. What happened to Melissa settled in that bad rocky place far beyond the realms of terrible, but what it did not do was to chase him away and off these streets because now these streets are all he has, they are where he had met and come to know her, and they are where he can continue to savour even the merest hint of that thing, whether it was love or something as close as bedamned to love, that they had once been so blessed to share. She is three years gone, but out here he can still feel their closeness, perhaps not to the flesh and bones of her, but at the very least to her ghost. That, at the very least, because she haunts this city now.

To his knowledge, there had been no funeral. They don't bother, generally, not for the likes of her, not unless a priest or church minister intervenes. Two men had come, police, but of a different variety than those who were already crowding the scene. Armed with a black nylon sack that zipped all the way up the front and shut with an ugly snap, there was nothing gentle or sympathetic about the way they gathered her up and loaded her into the back of their grey, windowless van, nothing even the least bit compassionate. One was black-skinned with a neatly-trimmed goatee beard and the other was white and wore very delicate wire-framed glasses, but essentially they were mirror images of one another. Large men, here to take care of some dirty business. They dressed the same, in dark grey overalls and heavy coats, and they pulled on gloves and bagged Melissa up like they were dealing with a spill of trash. Their faces registered nothing, which somehow made the whole act even worse. So, no funeral, or none that Johnny was aware of, but that was all right. Melissa had never been much for the business side of religion, though he knew that she did like to pray, that she did take comfort in it, not in a churchy sort of way or anything, but in her own manner of simply talking to God, asking him for things and giving thanks when thanks were due. No funeral, but dead was dead, no matter what sort of spin anyone tried to put on the deal. The morgue and then the crematorium, ashes to ashes, dust back down to the grainy fur of dust again.

Maybe it is because of the lack of finality, the ritual sense of closure that really only comes from standing in a church, crying through the words and then watching that boxed-up loved one slip down into the earth of a grave or be eaten up by the flames of a cremating furnace, that Melissa has refused to be chased entirely away. Wherever

Johnny walks now he sees her, there on the familiar corners or tucked up in certain doorways, shielding herself from yet more of that dog day Sunday morning wind, there and just as real as breathing while the shadows keep their depth. Always out of reach though, and gone at the very moment he risks a step of approach, banished out of teasing or out of terror. Melissa had always delighted in a game of teasing, and she had more than earned her right to fear. So either is understandable. There she is as she might have been on her prettiest day, until just as he is about to step within reach, she is gone from him, dissipating first to a frail, smoky outline and then down to nothing at all. His heart breaks without fail every single time it happens, yet he falls for the trick over and over, both because he is helpless to resist and because he is afraid that if he doesn't at least try then a day may come when she will vanish for good. The passing of time cannot so much as touch the ache of his loss, and because she feels so constantly near, the wound falls open and bleeds anew every day, but he tells himself that feeling pain is at least feeling alive, and that, apparently, is worth something.

He stays in the city and he walks the streets, without hurry in his step, and the only way that he can go on is by holding fast to the lie that he is just walking, not thinking about her or looking for her at all, even when he is. Lies are like crutches, now just as much as always.

Of course he understands that she is gone, dead, and that is clear in his mind as the very worst sort of fact because he was there, right there on the scene with the others when they found her after two entire days and nights of searching.

Her body had lain slumped in that doorway after a long and bitterly cold night, there and beaten down to nothing, with her clothes torn away to expose her harried, rail-thin frame all glassy-skinned from the exposure and the malnourishment and wretched beyond nightmares. Something bestial had found her in the darkness and ripped out her throat, and all around her shattered carcass the snow was a thick and filthy brown, polluted from its proper crimson hue by the sullen amber cast of a lonely nearby streetlight. That obscene shade of brown was the only colour of any note in a sullen after-dawn cracking open into a new day, this one yet another aimless middle-stop in that long line of dog days, with January beating vicious one-two combinations into the front end of February. He was there on hand to see all that, and he understands completely what that means, that she is gone and he will be forever alone, but knowing that doesn't stop the dreams. A man lost in the desert will dream of a drink of water and if he gives up the dream then he will die because there is no more reason to go on.

Whoever was responsible for butchering Melissa down to chump had been as neat as doily lace about his work, skilled to the point of perfection that only came with stone-hard practice. A man that good with a knife poses a genuine threat everyone, even to society's upper echelons. They'd look for him, the police would, not so much because he'd done what he had done to Melissa, but because of the very fact that he'd done this at all, that he was imbued with enough poison in his veins and hatred in his heart to be able to take up a tool designed for nothing more than the practical duties of slicing food and use it to carve apart a throat of living, gasping, pulsing flesh. As much as anything, what sickened and terrified everyone who had stepped close to that scene was that he'd had the stomach to do this all so thoroughly. There were no signs of a struggle, and the wounds were clean. Nothing had been ripped, not so much as a single seam or button from the victim's over-shirt.

With a monster like this one – and monster was not overkill as a description, not in this case – there would always be another morning waiting just up ahead to mirror this, perhaps a week or a month or two months from now, and then after that one, another and another and another, and so on. A monster such as the man who'd done this got himself off on killing, on going out and wandering the streets in search of just the right pathetic little soul, that tiny sprout of a woman still young enough but just on the turn towards stale. He'd walk, studying the faces of the passers-by and even more carefully the faces of those people who had to huddle beneath bridges and in doorways and in the many other dark places of the city, because it paid high dividends to be meticulous about this selection. As with Melissa, he would probably look to pluck his next target from among the homeless or the prostitute class, but sooner or later he'd be sure to work up an appetite for better flesh, and the chances were only improving that number whatever next-in-line could be someone who actually counted for something, that or perhaps the wife of someone like that. So they'd take pains to look, the police would, and they'd keep on looking, following the muddy amber-lit bloodstains first through the snow and then the slush and then through whatever came after, the winds of spring and the baking days of summer. They'd keep on looking until they caught up with their prize, only it was a mistake to ever believe that they were bothering to look because of what had just happened to one worthless piece of street trash. The police had stood around, securing the area back from the doorway with yellow-and-black warning tape, preserving the scene, taking their evidence photographs and talking about how fucked-up all of this was, about how far beyond belief it was that anyone could even bring themselves to touch one of these people, never mind do something like this to them. There were some real sick bastards in the world and no mistake.

The talk was not about Melissa, but about a slab of meat, something rank and odious and nothing at all like a child of God, not even related to the idea of a real person. And all of that unfolded while he stood there, watching and listening, in clear view but back a ways, in the mouth of a nearby alleyway, watching without being seen to watch, crying, but not in a way that anyone would bother to notice. The police saw evidence when they looked, Exhibit A, The Murder Victim; they saw arms and legs, tiny perished breasts coated with a crust of blood and dark staring eyes and a mouth open and clogged all the way to the back of the throat with gathered feathers of snow. What they missed and what they could never even imagine, was the notion of love attached to anyone like this. So they missed a lot.

He stood there, watching and waiting for something to happen, crying to fill the time until dawn had properly broken, and after a while he realised that the tears had stopped, that he had cried himself out and his throat had begun to throb with thirst for something the right sort of hot to drink – wine that would burn all the way down and touch the parts that most needed touching – and he allowed himself one last look, hoping that this would not be how he'd remember her, but knowing that as a memory, a mental image, it would never be far from his conscious thoughts. Then he turned away and set himself to walking. Not in any hurry, because there was no place along this street or the next or the one after that that would be any better or worse than where he was just then, out in the open with a dog day stirring awake and a sky above thick to the very heavens with snow. Not in a hurry, but moving just the same, walking, because movement felt right, felt like an answer, of sorts.

Now, three years and some change later, he is still walking, still moving. There are days when the answer seems very close, as close in fact as the ghost that he is always chasing, and there are other days, the dog day Sundays full of bitter cold and blowing wind, when he knows that he will never catch up, but that the chase is all he has and all he will ever have. Dog days when all the world feels weighted against him and when crying helps only a little and only for a while. Lately, he has taken to talking, and Melissa, who had always been such a good listener in life, is no less so now in death.

This isn't any kind of town for the likes of you, she used to say. Not for the likes of you.

She was correct about that but not all the way correct. He walks and watches her dance, her smiling face light again and full of love, happy with the movement of life. Then, just for a moment, he is caught up in a gust of fatigue, and he stops and closes his eyes, squeezes them shut, and sees her lying dead in that doorway, her pathetic breasts and stomach clotted with an apron of dried blood, brown at first, a dirty shade, but then, as the light slowly waxed, a colour of sickening maroon. Her eyes are wide with shock, her mouth yawning some feeble plea, and the only thing remotely resembling a smile now is that gaping black rictus grin of a throat wound as it gathers in the first stray spittle of the snowflakes. He is standing in a quiet city street with his eyes clenched shut, but in the swollen blackness of his mind he is really standing just a few paces away from that doorway, back with the other gathered watchers who are happy to gaze past the yellow-and-black warning tape and the shoulders of the policemen hunched against the cold, and no one bothers to notice him at all, even though he is crying, and even though his fingers are caressing the blade of a small knife that is concealed in his coat pocket, caressing until his touch grows heavy and the flesh is pierced. When he opens his eyes again to face the world, the morning seems to have lost a little of its edge. A gloom has settled, heavier than feels right. He takes a moment to study the street, taking in the familiar shapes of the crawling traffic, the granite and sandstone building fronts and the few unhurried passers-by. And ghosts too, just ahead, at that corner, or across the street in that boarded up doorway. He takes a deep, shuddering pull of breath and the fatigue falls away, leaving him, the perfect dog for this perfectly ugly Sunday morning, free to walk again, his destination nowhere.

SYZYGY

Melinda was leaving me.

'I doubt that either of us will ever forget today,' she said, over breakfast. The arrangements were already set, her new man, Jonathan, was coming by to pick her up at noon, and now that we'd reached the actual brink, a sort of calmness had settled over us.

She was referring to this business of the eclipse, of course, using the significance of one event to heighten that of the other. I wanted to say that we hardly needed anything as dramatic as a shifting of the heavens to help mark down today as a permanent memory, but one glance at her strangled the words in my throat and I busied myself instead with reaching for and buttering another slice of toast.

Everything worth saying had already been said, we'd laid out the apologies and the accusations, tossed and turned them until they were burnt through on both sides, and we both knew that there was no way on from here other than the way we were taking. Still, I suppose that there had to have been some good moments during our time together, and it was for the sake of those that we had wordlessly agreed to keep up this charade of acting like civilized human beings. Later, there would be all the time in the world for tears.

I could feel her watching me, watching the amount of butter I was using, but she let it go because I was no longer her fight. She sat across the table, her spoon troubling a bowl of sodden bran flakes, doing more poking than actual digging. She was wearing a blue-and-white tartan-patterned blouse, sleeveless, which made a nice boast out of her narrow body, and her hair was tied up in the way she knew I liked. She looked good. Better than good, great. I ate my toast and tried to forget that this morning's effort at alluring appearance was not for my benefit but for his.

'It's funny, don't you think, when you consider all those enormous planets and moons spinning about in all that space.'

Not ha-ha funny, but yeah, I suppose there is a bit of the Groucho about it.

'Space is empty and yet it's full of stars. How can that be? And this business of the eclipse, this one moment when our rock and another rock defy all that emptiness to line up exactly with a great flaming ball of gas, well, it puts in perspective how small our lives are, and how insignificant. Think about it; the next time this happens could be hundreds of years from now, maybe thousands. We'll be gone and forgotten, and all the arguments and the laughter will be gone, too. Christ, it's enough to make you go cold.'

I poured myself another half cup of coffee, then out of

spite helped myself to the last slice of toast. This time she watched me openly while I smeared on the butter.

'You should use the spread, you know,' she said, going delicate with her disapproval for the sake of the truce. I could feel the edge in her voice, though.

'Should I?' As serene as you like. I can be a bastard and a half when I set my mind to it.

But this morning she was beyond stepping into my traps. She dropped her spoon into her mess of bran and raised both hands in that gesture of surrender that made me want to bounce her off every wall in the room and at the same time to sweep her up into my arms and never let her go. 'Forget it,' she said. 'Your heart, your choice.'

I took a bite of toast, chewed it without enjoyment, then dropped the slice in favour of the coffee. She watched me until I met her stare and then she did something with her mouth, a little crimping of the lips that might have been a smile or might not, and she looked away. The tablecloth was bunched a little at the corner to her right, the material dragged out of shape by the weight of the coffee pot, and she fumbled to undo the ruffles and then ran a hand across the surface, as if to assure herself of the smoothness. The tablecloth was hers – she had chosen the style and design, white cotton with silver embroidered geese, quaint but pretty – but when it came to the matter of dividing the possessions she insisted that it remain here. She had no need for it, she said, and then, almost as if she'd been caught in a lie or some particularly sordid act, she mentioned that Jonathan's kitchen table was round rather than square. That seemed to imply something, though even now I can't quite figure out exactly what.

We sat there, passing the time with empty words and stolen glances. Then, finally, we heard the rumble of the car outside, and we both knew that it would be Jonathan, her new main man, a lumbering oaf who had somehow become the answer to all her problems.

'Look after yourself,' she said, in a small voice.

I almost made a witty riposte, but held back. She didn't deserve much, not after all that had happened, but she deserved that. I nodded. 'You can send that one to the bank,' I said, squeezing into a smile. 'From now on, it's number one all the way.'

In the hallway, I put a hand on the small of her back, leaned in and kissed her cheek almost at the lobe of her left ear. Jonathan was there all right, his too-big carcass squeezed into the coupé that looked both expensive and ridiculous. He sat there, tapping one bear's paw of a hand on the rim of the steering wheel, and my hand on Mel's back was to manoeuvre her out of his line of vision because the door was open. I didn't give a damn what he saw of me, but to my mind the very least that she deserved was the dignified privacy of a last farewell. After all, we'd just put paid to a whole life together, an entire convoluted history. We had reached the point now where our connection no longer counted for very much, but at this moment, with my lips pressed against the silken flesh of her cheek and with the tinge of her true scent scraping through the cloying breath of Christian Dior number whatever perfume, it felt, at least to me, as if we'd never known a greater intimacy. When she stooped to reach for her suitcase, the little nubs of her spine rose against my touch and a memory stormed my mind of our first time in bed together, back when everything was fresh and new, and exploring every inch of her body was a step further into the unknown.

'Take care of yourself,' she whispered, clearly not trusting the strength of her voice. A tear blistered the lashes of one eye and burst against the heel of her hand. I held my breath for the deluge, but it seems that I was only worth the one tear.

And then, without another word, she turned away and was gone.

I stood in the doorway for a long time. There was heat in the late August day, but nothing unbearable. A breeze stirred the alders that leaned over the wall of the nearby schoolyard, and traffic out on the main road was light for the hour. I studied the sky, expecting some kind of revelation, I think, but there was little to see, only a blanket of washed-out grey and away on the horizon the stately crawl of a high-altitude jet. Apart from the imminent eclipse, this was just another ordinary Tuesday. Time still puttered along at its usual rate, always chasing, always in debt. Billions of hearts across the map still leapt, ached and, in dozens of tragic ways, broke. The world hadn't stopped turning, hadn't even slowed.

Just after two o'clock, the dogs began to howl.

Earlier, when I'd gone out into the yard to feed them, I found them subdued, drained of their usual boundless energy. Their barks were sharp and catching, the unsettling screech of the youngest one starting off a rounded chorus amongst the others, and they all stood with backs arched, their heads hung low and their haunches all aquiver. Such behaviour was most unlike them. But when I set out their food and assured them with a few soft words and a quick pat, they bunched together and attacked their feeding bowls with something like their usual gusto, and it seemed that everything was all right again. Dogs have a lovely way of simplifying a situation.

I'd made myself a sandwich and was just sitting down to eat when the howling began. Such an eerie sound. I went outside and found them huddled together in one corner of the yard, all four of them. They raised their heads to howl and I'm not sure that I have ever experienced anything more unnerving. The sound seemed alien to them, an earthy long-ago sound, as forlorn as whale-song and as strange. They howled, and then shivered violently as, in answer, somewhere off in the distance, another dog started up with another series of long bleating whoops.

The sky looked unchanged, still the same blanket grey of earlier, though away to the west the cloud had begun to split apart and lay in flumes across a thin swath of blue. The little breeze of earlier had sighed itself out or fallen away and a peculiar stillness had overtaken the afternoon. I thought about going back inside, but didn't. Couldn't.

On last night's news, they had come up with the technical or scientific term 'Syzygy'; I had no idea what such a word actually meant, but standing in my yard, feeling the mystery of the day unfold around me, I found myself speaking it aloud over and over and delighted in its buzzing cadence and jagged lack of vowels. 'Eclipse' explained what was happening but 'Syzygy' went closer to truly defining this imminent celestial alchemy. I savoured the word and sang it in between long whistling breaths, until a little after half past two, at which point the thin darkness of a false night had more fully fallen.

Once it started, the eclipse quickly engulfed the sun. As such, there was nothing to see, not with the bank of cloud obliterating the magic, but then there was no real need to see. Over the next few minutes, the light was gradually sucked out of the day, and the air tingled. Whatever was happening kicked awake some sort of primal instinct, in me just as much as in the animals, and I made a conscious effort to focus on the details, on the reaction of the dogs, now whimpering and circling one another in a frenzy of confusion, on the bleached and then slowly dusky hue that overtook the colours of the world, on the rise in my own pulse rate and the stirring of something in my stomach that wasn't fear exactly, but wasn't so far off that either. The dying day, plunging from its apex, carried a genuine sense of event, marking this out as an occurrence of significant magnitude and, really, one quite beyond comprehension.

The ancients would have been mesmerised. They'd have been on their knees, worshipping and wailing, howling as the animals howled now, and those who had dared to look, the hooded druids or those of the warrior class, would have witnessed their godly sun devoured by a creeping blackness, eaten down to one final flash of desperation before all was lost. It was easy enough, at least for me, to picture the scene, to bear witness in mind if not in body to the wails climbing headlong to crescendo until there was no more hope of salvation except through prayer, or prayer and promise, the divulgence of a blood sacrifice, perhaps. Nowadays the mathematicians, astronomers and astrophysicists have a way of using a slew of formulaic babble to explain away every wonder known to mankind, their numbers over numbers multiplied by letters that allow their own gibberish brand of logic to prevail. But back when time was measured at different speeds, wasn't it possible that the survival of the whole world rested on some phrase uttered either by accident or with intent, or with a single pleading word dropped in amongst the veritable throng of assurances and incantations, even a word as spine-twisted and apocryphal as 'Syzygy', one hyped to the very brim with witchery and import? If we are asked to believe in such-and-such a chemical or the atomic balance of water, sand or salt, why can't we allow ourselves to believe that somewhere out in all that empty space there was and maybe still is something sufficiently godly and almighty just waiting for one word, one precious word or any word at all, to awaken its slumbering mercy? The ancients believed it, and by design or happenstance prayed the word that slowly, ever so painfully slowly, brought their sun bulging out through the darkness once again, their golden god renewed and reborn.

Today turned out to be a day of two dawns and after a few breath-held moments of weighty darkness, the eclipse began to wane. Any affinity that we might have shared with our aeons-gone ancestors was lost as Syzygy proved to be no more than a fleeting wonder, there and then gone, a life lived and lost in the span of a heartbeat. Maybe it served its purpose, though; maybe the almighty of the universe had heard me utter the magic word and had deigned, yet again, to comply, to let the sun have another chance at life.

Or maybe, as the scientists said, this was merely a natural phenomenon, a temporary confluence of the planets and stars. Whatever the reason, out beyond the obliterating smear of cloud, space continued on its merry way, worlds turned, and the sun broke free of its shadow-trap, one crack at a time.

White light sifted into the day and the darkness was broken down to twilight. Within a few minutes, unseen birds began to sing, tricked into concert by the sudden, unexpected return of day, and then the dogs settled and my backyard seemed to breathe with renewed vigour. After the darkness, everything seemed more vital and alive, colours appeared far more brilliant than before, even on an overcast late August afternoon.

I thought about Melinda and wondered if she was settling comfortably into her new life; if, with her new man at her side, she had stood at some window or in the middle of a garden space over on the other side of town to watch the unfurling of this astronomical sleight of hand. The idea of an eclipse would have appealed enormously to the old Melinda, the Melinda who had once upon a time loved nothing more than walking on storm-lashed beaches or watching the first arrival of the swallows, the Melinda who, a lifetime ago, had fallen headlong into love with me. But she had changed in a hundred years worth of ways over the past six months, ever since Jonathan had appeared on the scene to turn her head with his leery charm and to turn her mind on to all manner of small excitements. I estimated the odds lay probably better than evens that the newly matched lovers had foregone the wonders of Syzygy in favour of working through a bottle of celebratory champagne or enjoying a stint of bedtime acrobatics.

A day of two dawns, the day when life's road split in two. Now, she had gone and followed her path and I was left behind to stray blindly along on mine. I found or made time to go and stand in my backyard for the better part of an hour, time that I chose to spend watching the sky, watching for the least shift, the most delicate slip of the light. But what does that say about me? The sun, moon and planets did their best to keep me entertained, of course, even if their tricks were all turned behind a wall-thick curtain of cumulus and stratum, but while the whole Syzygy business was undeniably impressive, at least as a notion, it spanned too brief a time to be in any way truly world-shaking. As much as I tend to feel like one sometimes, out of pace as I am with society in general, I am not an ancient. I am me, just one of the innumerable tiny shards of pain stuck on a spinning speck of dust, trying in the only way I know how to exist, and like everyone else, I spend my days and nights denying my insignificance, struggling to think up some vague crumb of worth in order to justify every move I make, every fantastic thought I have. That's what living has become, at least in my corner of the world.

Too quickly, the darkness fell away and the day was bright again. The world was once more content to turn its face away from the whispers of magic and to settle instead for the stoicism of bill-paying and child-bearing, that state where equilibrium is everything and highlights are small and, generally, within reach; highlights such as the swirling beauty of a slow dance in a big room or the pure satisfaction of a steak dinner. If joy and misery are opposite sides of the scale, balance is to be found with the banal. Contentment really is worth its weight in gold.

Like Mel, I found myself free to go where I wanted and to follow my heart's desires. What I chose to do was to go back inside and to sit and eat the sandwich I'd earlier made and then abandoned. The bacon would be cold by now, the fat beginning to congeal. Which, actually, was just how I like it.

LITTLE INDIGNITIES

In the old days, every village in the country had a man like Paudie O'Reilly in their midst. Standing at just a shade under six feet in height and with the heavy, rounded shoulders of someone well versed in the distribution of casual violence, he was a brutal sort, all John Wayne swagger but without any of the dignity, boorish in everything he did and said.

Before the years slowed his bones, when his tight winding would unravel with the least provocation and his aura of menace was still actively deserved, he played out his rage-games in late-night brawls after the pubs had let out. His blood inflamed by the sting of whiskey, he'd stand tall and wide in the road and draw deep of the darkness, filling his lungs for battle and sucking in murmured words, combing them for the least imagined slight. Everything back then was a trigger, an invitation to war, and his fists chased faces to smash like they were prizes at a funfair.

The passing of time saw his reactions slow and his once-refined bulk descend into a slothful fat, but his bitterness remained undimmed. To compensate for losing his physical threat, he cultivated a technique of verbal intimidation as a means of venting the explosive side of his nature. He was still a big man and hard-earned reputations faded very slowly. He had few friends, but he enjoyed the way people seemed to wilt in his company, the way they offered placating salutes and cleared his path whenever he strolled through the village, the way they paid silent attention when he held court at the counter down in Daisy Forde's public house, laughing like idiots whenever he bothered to crack a joke and cheering him on when, towards the end of the night and after drinking his fill of stout, he'd rock back in his chair and belt out a rendition of 'The Stone Outside Dan Murphy's Door', the only song he knew all the way through that didn't feature some heroic deed attributable to the IRA.

They talked behind his back, of course. Women especially, but men too, and a single glance at his wife provided evidence enough that his tyrannical ways didn't cease at the doorstep. Maggie was a frail, wizened creature, with large pale green eyes fixed eternally to some desperate middle distance and a West Cork brogue that fluttered in singsong gasps through her whisper of a voice. Everyone recalled how, during the early years of the marriage, the night-time would ring out with screams of pain and a most terrible pleading to please stop, that she was sorry and it would never happen again, whatever it was that she was supposed to have done, however little a thing. The thick pebble-dash walls of the terraced home muffled his growling replies, but that somehow only added to their sense of menace. Passers-by would stop to listen, neighbours would fill doorways and emerge head and shoulders from windows. They'd swap knowing glances and feel a mixture of disgust and helplessness, until finally the screams would subside to the small, heartbroken moans of a thoroughly defeated soul, and unable to bear it a moment longer they'd shrug and hurry on their way or slip back inside their homes, understanding that the situation was beyond their control and there was nothing they could do to help or interfere.

The vagueness that marked out Maggie from most of the other women in the village was a necessary survival mechanism, her way of dragging herself through yet another day. She'd miss the essence of questions and comments, wander past people without even noticing their smiles of greeting, and was easily startled by even the most friendly touch. 'Beaten stupid,' was how the women described her condition, and they always spoke of it in sympathetic tones, their way of giving thanks to the Almighty that they had been spared such an existence.

The pairing of Paudie and Maggie was the very definition of opposites attracting, and seemed a mockery, a collusion between the most wicked elements of fate. Silly with youth and headlong in a delusion she had mistaken for love, Maggie's living nightmare had started out as a simple dream of happiness. At seventeen, she knew nothing of life beyond the soothing tedium of rural village ways, of milking her father's cows and feeding the hens, of helping her mother around the house with the endless chores of cooking and cleaning, of filling the little spare time she could find with sewing and some light reading before the hour grew too late and her eyes grew sore and weary from the stammering of the candle's flame as it wrestled to hold its shape against the dozen whistling draughts.

He had bounded into Ballinascarty as part of the Post & Telegraph Company crew, Paudie O'Reilly, ten years her senior, the flesh of his face burnt russet from exposure to a salt-riven sea breeze and the hottest summer anyone could ever recall. The small, close set of his eyes surveyed everything with a calm that veered in and out of scorn. At the céili that first Friday night in September he had been brazen in his approach, elbowing his way through the idling packs of local youths and with the beckoning gesture of an open hand luring her out onto the floor. Trembling with excitement and anticipation, she imagined grace in his lumbering swagger, and she fought against swooning as he danced her to a frenzy, his breath reeking of porter, his strong hands spinning her around until she was light-headed and swept off her feet. He leaned in close again and again so that there was nothing to breathe but his own stale air, and his voice rumbled through the drone of a fiddled reel, telling her she was the most beautiful creature that he had ever seen. Like a flower in bloom, he said, his life's single attempt at poetry. She knew that she wasn't beautiful, because the small rust-speckled square of her father's shaving mirror had told a plain, uncompromisingly truthful story, but that night, dressed in her best skirt and her sister's blue cardigan, and spun until she was dizzy with happiness, she held onto his words and savoured them.

When the dancing was done, he stood to his fullest height and smiled in an open-mouthed way that revealed small grey teeth. His skin gleamed with sweat and even the heavy slathering of brilliantine had not been enough to control the wild flay of his jet-black hair. As soon as they had left the brightly lit hall behind, he wove his fingers into hers, and she felt as small and vulnerable as a bird. They kept a slow pace in the darkness, and he talked in a low grumble that seemed to rise up from the ground, a barely controlled roar that throbbed and ached to be let loose, about his own village, Douglas, and what a grand place it was. He told her about his job with the Post & Telegraph and how it had taken him all over Munster, but that in all his travels he had never yet seen a woman as fine as her. She, who had always been considered a girl, was glad of the night's help in concealing her blushes. They walked slowly, leaning into the hill, and at the front gate there was an awkward moment when he suddenly plunged his face toward hers. A spout of panic threatened to overtake her and she was certain that she'd smother or that she'd scream out in discomfort from beneath the forceful crush of his chin and cheekbones, but she fought hard against the negatives, closed her eyes and told herself how lovely this was, her first kiss, her first romance, and with the strongest man that she had ever known.

A week or so later, he was gone, taken off in some other direction by the demands of his job, but from time to time over the next six months or so he'd arrive unannounced, armed with a bag of boiled sweets or with a small bunch of posies or daffodils wilting in his clenched fist, and he'd say just the right things to feed her addiction. The time that spun between his visits helped their relationship, allowing her to endlessly reconstruct their moments together until they meshed perfectly with her fantasy. And then, early in the new year, he produced a ring, an old sliver of tarnished gold that had belonged, he said, to his grandmother. It hung loosely on her finger but that didn't matter, because the answer was yes. Having spent a childhood so sheltered from all the world's cruel vagaries, she easily missed, or else chose to overlook as insignificant, the first corrupting signs of a dream shifting into the realms of nightmare.

She'd been foolish, but all in the name of love, and plenty had made that irrevocable mistake. The first time he hit her he'd been drunk, had stumbled in late from celebrating a great Douglas hurling victory over the Rockies. He hit her the same way that he hit men outside Daisy Forde's pub and only the fact that she had been rising from the chair and was therefore off balance at the moment of impact saved her from a broken nose or possibly worse. Still, the blow had been enough to streak the late hour with flames of pale light, and her sinuses flushed so quickly with the cloying tang of blood that she was certain she'd choke. She cried out and cupped her hands beneath her face in a futile effort to staunch the spill and protect her blouse from staining. He followed her as she stumbled through to the bedroom, his lumbering gait careening off walls and furniture, slurring threats about someone named Burke and that next time he'd kill her stone dead if he caught her so much as looking crooked at anyone. When he fell on her there was nothing to do but let him finish and try not to annoy him too much by crying. And when, the following day, he apologised for what had happened, he sounded so sincere and so strangled with guilt and self-loathing that she really wanted to believe it was the influence of the drink which had caused him to hit her. Many before her had made that mistake too. Love was stupid as well as blind.

Years passed slowly and there was no salvation to be found in anything except retreat. She learned to sleepwalk through her days, to pack away her grief and to take the bruises and the broken bones as penance for her foolishness in walking so blindly into this life. On the single occasion that she tried to seek solace by confiding in her mother, she was told that she had made her bed and there was nothing to be done. That day, seated at the kitchen table of the farm-house in which she had been reared, she sobbed while her mother looked on without sympathy for her predicament. When her father came in from the fields she had wanted to tell him too, but even when her mother went outside to the well for water to make tea the necessary words just refused to offer themselves.

Less than a fortnight later, she suffered a miscarriage. She was thirteen weeks into her pregnancy when she collapsed in the garden and the new life that she was carrying flushed out onto the dirt of the yard. Lying in bed during the days and nights immediately after, she let her mind vie between competing lines of thought: the fantasy of how her child would have been, how beautiful and perfect once born and fully grown, and the reality of precisely which punch or kick had committed the heinous act of murder. Neighbours who visited told her that no one was to blame. She did her best to smile because she understood that they meant well, but there was blame here and everyone knew it. This was all her fault. She had married a brute, too stupid to know better, stupid for believing the notion that love was not the world's biggest and filthiest lie. In her hunger to be wanted, she had looked at yellow and saw only blue. Paudie had led her on a merry dance, had filled her head with nonsense and had made her feel alive. Now it was Paudie's hands that had dragged her by the hair from her place at the table, Paudie's feet which had kicked her unborn baby to death as she lay curled in a protective ball on the cold flagstone floor. But it was she herself who had embraced a life sentence. Unaware of the damage that had been caused to her insides, the neighbours patted her gently on the shoulder as she lay in the bed that she had made and earned, her small, brutalised frame propped up with pillows and surrounded by days-old unread newspapers, and they told her not to let this get her down, that she was little more than a child herself and there'd be plenty of time for bearing children. They meant well when they said that these things happened sometimes and that questioning them was flying in the face of God, but by then Maggie had learned more than her share of lessons, and she knew in her heart that God was just as much a fable as the hellish joke of love or happiness.

The chore of ironing could induce a trance that was often close to unbreakable. Paudie was very particular about his shirts, and Maggie knew better than to rush the process. The humid air created a different world, one that almost begged of her to dream. Lately, her mind was quick to find direction, dreaming up a home on a hill, a place for her alone, with high ceilings, thick carpet on the floors and paintings on the walls. Maybe a couple of acres so that she could keep a horse, an old bay gelding that, for no particular reason, she'd name Cooper and who wouldn't be much to look at, certainly no thoroughbred, but who'd have the heart of a warrior. On a place like that she'd need no one, not Paudie, not her family.

The banging at the door seemed miles away, a flutter no more noticeable than the small ceaseless clapping of a bluebottle bounding over and over against the glass of the pantry window, and easy to ignore. Easy until it became more pronounced, and until the voices carried through from the road. Carefully, she set down the iron. A sense of unease washed through her, but that may have been nothing more than reflex, the reaction she had developed upon hearing her husband's nightly return, and she had long since braced herself against the impact of such feelings. He'd be drunk again, of course, too drunk to even manage an unlocked door, and she hoped that whoever he had brought home with him from the pub would be the kind of men that knew, even in that state, how to behave themselves.

There was a moment, upon opening the door, when she actually believed that he was dead. It looked that way, his great frame sagging between the set of two struggling men, the thin white ropes of his remaining hair corkscrewing wildly from his lowered head, his knees bent with weakness, his boots dragging on their toes.

'We all thought he was just drunk,' one of the men was saying, pronouncing the words slowly as though he was fishing them from distant memory. 'He fell off the stool with an awful clatter and we couldn't wake him.'

Maggie pictured the scene; Paudie holding sway on some favoured topic, a pint of stout clenched in one sweeping fist, those eyes blazing, daring anyone to interrupt or contradict him. Maybe the grumble of his voice as he broke into song. And then the fall. On sleeping feet, she shuffled aside and watched the men as they struggled to carry her husband up the step and into the house, stumbling to navigate the narrow hallway, one groaning with the strain of such a weight, the other through clenched teeth hissing a few slurred words of comfort meant probably for anyone who wanted them. They stretched him out on the bed and Maggie thanked them, not really knowing what else to say or do. Both of these men had, over the years, been regular visitors to her home, guests of Paudie's, usually after the pubs had shut, hangers-on eager to slake the last of their thirst from the dregs of a whiskey bottle, but neither of them were from Douglas and at that moment, try as she might, she could not recall their names. For a few seconds they stood there staring at her, trying to weigh the situation through the fog of their drunkenness. Then, instinctively aware that there was to be no offer of further drink, they took their leave, reluctantly, muttering the usual promises that they'd call in tomorrow to see the patient and that if there was anything they could do she need only ask.

With great care, Maggie unlaced her husband's boots, then turned them, first one and then the other, towards the window. In the pale yellow light of a low-slung conch moon, she surveyed the damage, confirming with her fingertips the full extent of the scuffing. Polish would cover the worst of it she decided with a sigh. Then she undressed and climbed across Paudie's inert body to her own side of the bed. She lay there for a while, her eyes closed but the wash of the moonlight through the window still brightening her thoughts. She felt very small, almost childlike, and after some interminable length of time she drifted off into a light sleep, soothed by the scrape of laboured breathing beside her.

By morning, it was clear that something was very wrong. Paudie had not moved in the night; he lay there on the bed sheets, still dressed but for his boots, his breath still rattling in shallow heaves, his face sagging from the depths of a stony coma. Maggie shook him gently and his head lolled leftwards, revealing a black crust of blood that had seeped from his ear and down onto the pillow. She screamed, a sound that seemed to come from somewhere beyond her body. The world dimmed, just for an instant, and she had to steady herself against the bedroom wall to keep from passing out. The blood was a molten puss, with the thick, clammy texture of treacle, and her first thought was that his shirt was ruined, that she'd never manage to get such a stain from his collar.

After a few minutes Dan Hartnett from next door arrived at the window, his wife Kathleen at his side. He tapped at the glass, said that they thought they had heard a scream and asked if anything was wrong. Everything came apart then. Violent sobs tore from her, rocking her body. Kathleen held her, gently, as though afraid that a strong embrace might inflict serious damage. Then the worst of the shock subsided and through stuttering gasps she told them how Paudie had been brought home and how she had dismissed it as just too much porter. God knew it wouldn't have been his first time passing out drunk. She hadn't realised it was something more serious until she saw the blood. They listened, nodding in sympathy, then led her out of the bedroom and sat her in the old armchair by the empty fireplace. Kathleen stayed with her, holding her hand, trying to whisper words of solace that felt hollow and sounded worse. Dan hovered unsure what to do. Then, finally, he drifted outside, and within an hour an ambulance arrived, drawing up outside the door with sirens wailing.

Paudie had suffered a stroke. The doctor who explained the situation was a tall, slender man with a long narrow face and hangdog eyes, and when he introduced himself Maggie had been too distracted to catch his name. She thought it might have been either Brown or Bowen. He was elderly, or appeared so, and he dressed in a dark suit of some material made shiny with age. A white carnation bloomed on his left lapel, looking ludicrously out of place with the sepia tones of the hospital surround. He showed Maggie to a seat then moved behind his desk and considered her openly. She had a sense that he was helping himself to the secrets of her soul, and when he spoke his voice had the soft, gently indefinable quality of smoke.

'The night spent drinking probably masked any early warning signals, Mrs O'Reilly. From the tests we have carried out, it appears that your husband had a minor stroke first. You said that the men he was drinking with told you he had fallen from his barstool? That would be in fitting with a small aneurysm. A sudden numbness or weakness down one side, dizziness, the loss of balance or co-ordination.

Of course, the problem is that such symptoms can also be caused by inebriation, which is probably why no one even thought to send for medical help. Later, we believe that he suffered a major stroke, some time during the night. The blood was caused by a haemorrhage, though even if he had been in hospital when that happened it would have been very unlikely that we could have offered anything in the way of prevention. I'm afraid that there is extensive damage, with little or no hope of improvement. We do believe that mentally he is almost unharmed, though whether one would choose to see that as a blessing or a curse, giving the long-term prognosis, is really a matter of opinion, I suppose.'

He paused, set his mouth in a shape he adjudged to be most sympathetic. 'You mustn't reproach yourself for any of this, Mrs O'Reilly. Sometimes these things just happen.'

'He's only forty-seven,' Maggie whispered into the handkerchief that she held bunched in her small fist. 'That's no age at all.' As if those few words of argument ridiculed this entire business.

It was the new year before Paudie was allowed home, and the better than three months spent confined to a hospital bed had reduced him to a fragile shell, a vague imitation of the man he had once been. Bound to a wheelchair parked almost permanently in the open doorway, held upright by a packing of pillows and wrapped in old woollen blankets against the cold spring air, he gazed mutely out at the goings-on of the village but seemed separate from it all, beyond the touch of that former life. Amusement and rage registered without note across his face, the sucker-punch of his brainstorm having so disfigured his features, wrenching his mouth agog, ripping the sight from one eye, slumping his once formidable shoulders, that it became impossible for him to express himself. At first, neighbours took a few minutes out of their day to offer some friendly words of chat, generally confining themselves to the usual light-hearted banter about the weather or the hurling, but also making mention of how much better he was looking and how he'd be his old self again in no time at all, they were sure of it. But any effort at consolation felt hollow, so one-sided that spoken aloud the words took on the characteristics of a taunt, and after a while it felt like a better option simply to wave and hurry along, better for everyone.

Weeks after his return home, Maggie was spoon-feeding him from a bowl of potatoes mashed in buttermilk when the pulped food went against his breath and he began to choke. Hunched sideways in his chair he struggled for air, barking out coughs as his face turned a sad shade of puce. There was nothing to do but sit and watch, and after a minute or so the horror of what she was seeing began to fade. While his bulging eyes blistered with tears from the strain, Maggie gently patted his hand and waited, accepting her helplessness and giving in to a little smile of sympathy, while things took their natural course. And when the worst of the struggle passed and he found his breath again, she wiped his mouth and chin with an old tea towel, kissed his forehead and told him that she was sorry for feeding him so hurriedly but that she just had so much to do around the house. Sweat cut runnels down his swollen cheeks, and he hunched there, a bleating wreckage, while she promised that she'd be more careful in the future. But no matter how diligent she tried to be, the choking fits became a feature of mealtimes, often growing so bad that she had no choice but to prize open his mouth and use her fingers to scrape the food morsels from his tongue and throat. The choking was a side effect of the stroke, she told Kathleen Hartnett, one of those terrible things that simply couldn't be avoided. 'He has to eat or he'll just waste away.'

For Maggie, the whole world had changed. After years of living a plastic life, consumed by fear at every turn and every uttered word, she suddenly found herself with the freedom to do as she pleased. Paudie sat in his chair all day, and when he wasn't gazing out at the village from his doorway prison, he'd wordlessly watch as she attacked the chores of washing, cleaning and cooking. What he must have seen was the terror that he had once pummelled into her gradually replacing itself with the confidence of knowing that it was she now who held the upper hand of power. She controlled the household and in his disabled state he lost his air of menace and became vulnerable and weak, relying completely on her to feed and clothe him, to wash him and to keep him alive.

To anyone looking in from the outside, she appeared a dutiful and dedicated wife, constantly tending to his many needs and demands without a single uttering of complaint. She had long since stopped looking after herself and caring about her appearance, and that didn't change now that she had been presented with the opportunity for improvement. Her hair still hung mousy and lank across her face and shoulders, roughly clipped by her own hand to an uneven but perfunctory shape, and she still wore the threadbare skirts and pinafores that she found in the cheapest baskets of the second-hand shops along North Main Street and the Coal Quay. She still looked haggard and frail, weary to the very bone from her sleepless nights and her long days of toil, and her eyes and mouth were fringed with deeply etched cobwebs of wrinkles, tattoos of the strain under which she lived. Those who gave her situation even a second of thought supposed that the years of marital cruelty had damaged her comprehension, that she had slipped into a perverse state of punch-drunk love, a victim addicted to her captor, but in their hearts they had to commend her just the same for the selfless loyalty that she showed towards a man who scarcely deserved such care.

On Sunday mornings she could be seen wheeling him up through the village to mass, and she took a place on the outer edge of a back row pew and held his hand while the priest, Fr Mulcahy, murmured prayers and gave thanks for the little that everyone had. Paudie was never what could have been considered devout in the observance of his faith, but the idea that he needed whatever solace and comfort prayer could bring did make perfect sense to people. When Fr Mulcahy mentioned from the pulpit that even the most wretched soul could find redemption through the words of Christ, more than a few among the congregation pictured Paudie as the prime example. And after mass had finished, Maggie lingered outside or, if it was raining, in the church's porch, to share some small-talk with the other parishioners and thank them for their good wishes. She smiled like a believer edging towards zealotry when she stated that she could see a definite improvement in her husband's health, that he had always been a strong man and he'd need to use every ounce of that same strength now to bear this cross. The women nodded and praised her for the work she was doing, while Paudie sat between them, staring into space, his face mangled into a grimace.

Rushing his food was a small mode of torture that led to other things, little indignities that stoked Maggie's sense of dominance. On cold nights she would set his chair in the room's furthest corner, far away from the fire so that the flames would tease him without offering any of their benefit. She insisted on washing him twice a day, morning and night, always from a dish with the water set close to boiling, and she scrubbed him roughly with a flannel cloth, all the while singing songs that she knew irritated him, Christmas songs in summer, or Frank Sinatra and Bing Crosby ballads, while his scalded skin made him moan in pain. She served him tea that was far too hot to swallow, holding the cup to his lips so that he had to take it all at once, and when she clipped his toenails she always made sure that the blades of the scissors nicked the tender flesh beneath the nail. And for hours at a stretch she would busy herself with cleaning the windows or scrubbing down the front step, steadfastly ignoring him even when the cloying stench of excrement announced that he had soiled himself. Sometimes she would leave him sitting unattended until nightfall, and when she'd strip off his clothes she'd find even the flesh of his back clammy with his own filth. Any guilt she felt over acting in such callous ways was nothing more than a light fluttering in her stomach, almost identical to a stirring of excitement, and easily enough ignored. She'd smile at Paudie, a smile she perfected a little more with each offering, and sing out an apology, maybe plant a kiss on his forehead and explain that she was just so busy, what with one thing and another, and surely he saw that, but of course she'd do her very best, her absolute damnedest, to ensure that it would not happen again. His eyes were the same small pale eyes that had fixed their sights on her back in the Ballinascarty céili hall on that long-ago Friday night, narrowly set and gleaming still, but with a ferocity that could only be dreamed of now. The love was gone, if it had ever been there at all, or had ever been anything more than lust mistaken for something fine, but a certain wisdom was in evidence now, an understanding of what exactly was happening to him, and why.

Occasionally, the district nurse would stop by to visit, and Maggie would stand there and watch while the usual cursory examinations were carried out. She never tried to explain away the bruises or abrasions except to say that Paudie could be a real handful at times, especially when dragging him into his chair or lifting him into bed. The nurse nodded, understanding, and murmured how hard it must be, having to bear such a burden. There were places, she said, over a cup of tea at the kitchen table, after Paudie had been dressed again and placed in his usual doorway position, places where trained staff would look after him. It would be a respite for both of them, because no man wanted to be such a trial to his loved ones.

Maggie sipped her tea and smiled. 'No,' she said, 'he

needs me and I need him. I can't give him up to strangers. And that's all there is to it.'

Time brought nothing but a kind of immunity. Maggie came to accept her shows of wickedness and, in the same way, Paudie found some way of handling the pain. If conscience could become callused, then so too could resolve. Soon enough, Maggie found that she needed something more to sate her appetite for revenge than the little pinch-and-twist indulgences of snagging his flesh with her chewed nails as she dressed him, or forcing him to consume all the things he hated until he began to gag and vomit in response, or leaving him to sit sodden in his own urine for entire days until his groin and inner thighs shone with the bright pink of yet another angry rash. When such cruelties began to lose an element of their glow, she raised the stakes, freshened them all over again by taking time to announcing exactly what little savagery she planned to inflict on him next. First in whispers, her mouth almost lovingly close to his ear so that memories of when they had been newlyweds could not help but flash through his stubborn mind, and then, when even that began to lose its lustre, in a calm, terribly logical voice that had never been hers.

'Time for your wash, my love. I do hope that the water won't be too hot for you this time.' Or: 'I have a special dinner for you today, Paudie. Raw sausages. Good for the bowels, they say.' Mute apart from the small moaning cry that was the reaction to the very worst of his misery, there was nothing Paudie could do or say to help himself.

And life would have continued on for both of them in

such a way, an endless game of cat and mouse, had death not interceded. Maggie awoke to a perfect July dawn with the sense that something irrevocable had occurred. Beside her in the bed, Paudie lay stiff as stone, but the atmosphere of the small bedroom felt unnaturally still and it took a moment for her to realise that the oddness was due to silence.

Since the stroke, Paudie's breathing had been a constant struggle, a cold nasal whistle straining in spurts through the sack of useless muscle and bone. It had become part of the noise of her day, and her night, an expected detail of her surround and a music so in tune with their lives that it required neither noticing nor recognition. She found herself waiting in the gossamer-thin half-light of the hour, huddled beneath the veil of a cotton sheet, her own breath a clot of terror in her throat. On the bedside locker the alarm clock pulsed to an impossibly slow time, a clack of seconds that had to be running slow, and she closed her eyes and gave in to her fear, letting the rush of melancholia wash over her like a blast of breeze.

He looked better in death than he had at any time since the stroke. All the neighbours said so. It was an ease to him, they said, their voices held low out of respect for the dead, an end to his suffering and to hers. Laid out on the bed, dressed in his best suit and with his hair swept back in a dignified way, he found again some of the physical dominance that had once made him such a distinctive figure. The stroke had scarred him, twisted his face, but they had been able to manipulate the relaxed muscles into a better shape. The years fell away and he looked almost young again.

The women carried trays of ham sandwiches and bracks already cut in slices and thickly buttered; the men brought bottles of stout. After the priest had been, someone produced a flagon of poteen and a glass was pressed into Maggie's hand, her fingers folded tight around it. 'Medicinal,' they told her, and she sipped at it, tasting nothing. 'It'll do you the world of good.' Perched on a hard-backed chair beside the unlit fire, she turned inward to find isolation from the pack. She was fortyish and old far beyond her time. Now she was also alone in the world, and not quite destitute perhaps, but hardly comfortable, either. Her mind refused to focus; every time someone asked a question of her, or every time she tried to set herself to a small chore, pouring some drinks, perhaps, or making another pot of tea, memories of Paudie stormed her mind, so completely that it became difficult to know for certain what was happening now and what was only remembered or imagined. There were details of him that she had somehow overlooked but saw with perfect clarity now: his diligence in and, appetite for, work; his self-belief; his handsomeness in a certain light. In her unconscious she supposed that she had always known these details, and that they had probably played a part in why she had fallen in love with him all those years before, why she had put up with so much misery and heartbreak during their time together. The sins lived on, some of them so terrible that she could never forgive them, but it wouldn't have done to ignore his qualities, not on this day, such a day for reflection. Qualities that, while not immediately obvious, even to her, were not insubstantial either.

She sat on her chair, taking the offers of condolence with a little bow of her head. The trembling that had been inside her for as long as she could recall finally made it obviously to the surface, and a cup of forgotten tea tumbled from her fingers to smash on the kerb of the fireplace.

Eventually the hour grew late and the party lost much of its enthusiasm, and in slow processions the neighbours said their so longs and drifted away, back to their own lives. When the last of them had gone, she stood and moved to the doorway of the bedroom. Empty, it seemed unfinished. She moved to the bed and perched on its edge, the thin mattress sagging beneath her. A feeling of desolation tugged at her mind, a throng of questions as to what she would do now, how she expected to survive, how she'd cope, a worn-to-ribbons forty-year-old, and all alone now, really for the very first time in her life. She felt the doubts dragging at her, wanting to bring her down, but with effort she shook them off. A smile turned the corners of her mouth and she yielded right of way. It was late now, moving on for midnight, but she had all the time in the world to sleep. There was some whiskey left and for now she felt like sitting a while at the fire. Maybe, she thought, feeling the first bubble of laughter tickle her mouth, she'd even raise her glass and drink a toast, to all the things she'd lost, and to life.

MORE THAN ONE
WAY TO SKIN A CAT

Perhaps he won't notice, the girl thought. After all, meat is meat, and he's an old man now, not as sharp as he once was. Not that she had ever known him to be especially sharp, but still, time had to count for something, didn't it? Time wore away mountains, they said. And meat is meat.

I have a mind for rabbit, he said. Fried in butter. A craving like you wouldn't believe. But he'd never know the difference, not in his state.

She'd take pleasure in this. Ever since she was a child, he'd been a cruel bastard. All for her own good, of course; that was how men like him always justified themselves. There are right ways to do things and wrong ways, he used to say, and the wrong ways will get your hands beaten blue. Better to learn that lesson now than later.

He used a switch to inflict the bruises, twenty slender inches of willow limb that he cut with ritualistic verve every Sunday afternoon while the echo of the priest's morning words still rang in his ears and his heart and blood still pounded with gospel piety. There was only so much beating to be had from a willow stick, and Sunday was the only suitable day for doing such holy duty. After ordering her to stand and watch from inside the crumbling backyard wall, he'd work his way across the rocky slope to where the willows grew. And once among them he'd take his time, his gnarled hands grasping and bending the low-hanging branches to test for the requisite give. A good switch needed to be at once strong and slender. There was no need for hurry and, depending on the time of year, he could take as long as ten or fifteen minutes before finally emerging again into the clearing. There he'd stand, in profile to his granddaughter's watching eyes, heedless of rain or wind, and he'd flay the air ten, twenty, thirty times with the newly-cut rod, this week's winner. The whining hiss produced by all that slashing made for a wicked song, but if so much as a single note failed to satisfy his critical ears, he'd toss the stick away and go back into the copse of trees to choose another, and another, until he found one to fit his towering standards.

In recent years he'd beaten her less, but that was due mainly to a combination of his growing old and her own heightened caution. She rarely spoke, except when to not speak would invoke his rage, and she hurried about the chores, the cooking, the cleaning and the many other small but necessary tasks that filled up her days. She read his constantly swinging moods and tried to step delicately around them. But back when she was just a child, he was more liberal with the stick, and more able. And Sunday nights were always the most dangerous time of the week for her, because he would be yearning to use the switch on flesh, and any excuse would suffice. Crying did no good; deaf to her desperate pleas, he'd announce the number of lashes that he adjudged to reasonably fit her latest misdemeanour: six for spilling the drinking water or for overcooking supper, ten for talking out of turn, a round dozen for whatever he would decide constituted a show of disobedience, and he'd keep on, tears or no tears, singing along to each scream of the switch in a deathly slow count-up until the sentence had been fully met and his own hungers sated.

She'd earned the right to hate him.

Now he was dying, and he wanted rabbit. The girl had known of his condition for weeks, ever since the racking cough had turned from a constant, tinny scraping sound into a pitiful bark that dripped wetly down into the white bristles of his chin. He'd felt something shifting far down inside, he said, and no drawn breath came easily after that. He was forced to spend much of his time in bed, his increasingly emaciated frame swaddled in four or five heavy grey blankets, so desperate was he to catch and hold on to even a modicum of elusive heat, but even in his brittle state he insisted on rising for an hour or two every day so that he might sit at his fireside and feel halfway like a man again. It was all that he had left to make him happy, he said, and while the fire blazed away at some kindling and a dried clod of turf, he'd sit in the half-light of the dying October days, smoking cheap cigars, consequences be damned, and reading and rereading his own grandfather's tattered copy of the Bible. Whenever he called out the girl's name, she put aside what she was doing to come and stand in the doorway and to listen while he unfurled whichever passage had set his imagination to flaming and now just had to be shared in a declaration as loud and glorious as any hosanna. His voice, though, was a worn nub, ravaged by time and lack of free use, and it tainted the words, even the beautiful words of Jesus, and words that might have been written with men like him very much in mind, those most in need of saving. The messages of the Gospels fell from his stub-toothed mouth with all their clemency chewed and gummed away, ruined of any good, to sound instead like condemnations and promises of hell. And after he was finished reading he held his granddaughter in a bloodshot gaze so that their recently reversed roles meant nothing and he was again the dominant force of the household. His body may have been withering steadily down to dust, but in his eyes the ferocity remained intact, and he stared, daring her to react, yearning for some small blanch that would require yet another lesson. The switch was gone, and the hands now were incapable of delivering even the least blow, but still the girl could not deny her terror. The smile warping her face, a gag that showed off a lower row of crooked yellow teeth, she held knuckles of breath high in her throat and waited for another coughing fit to bring him down, some stab of pain that would haul his stare away. Yes, he was dying, but some scars ran deep beneath the skin.

Set a snare, he said. Set a few, just to make certain. Will you, love?

He had to ask now, but he still wasn't asking. Not really.

She nodded that she would, of course she would, glad of this excuse to get outside. She knew of at least a couple of busy runs, the best of them down towards the bottom of the mountain, down where the ground held more soil and where great swathes of furze were able to thrive. And who knew, maybe she'd find him dead when she returned. Sometimes, thinking about that eventuality, she felt that she'd like to be there, to see the whole business through and to see the shadow of fear brushing across his face. But at other moments she found herself hoping that she'd be down in the village when it finally happened, or out gathering berries, or on the other side of the world. Because what if death really wasn't the end? What if it only took you out of one state and dropped you into another? She hurried through the house, gathering what she needed: the old man's pocket knife, a small pair of pliers, a coil of steel wire and a ball of strong twine.

There was still an hour of light left in the day. The stiff westerly breeze carried the cold, clean hint of approaching rain but, apart from some discomfort, it would make no real difference to the task at hand.

When she reached the low part of the mountain she paused to catch her breath and to properly survey the terrain. The furze dressed the land just above, the mesh of branches and spine-tipped leaves dark yet without their yellow blossoms, and it took less than a minute to identify the nicely flattened track that swept down to where the ground evened out and wandered through the long grass into a trim of briar and blackthorn. After just a little deliberation, she decided that the best place to lay her traps was just where the run narrowed before it led into the cover of the trees. Then she went to work at selecting and cutting branches to secure the snares, sinking their sharp edges deep into the pliant ground at varying intervals, cutting lengths of wire and twisting them into secure loops, setting up the taut nooses some five inches or so above the ground. This was a busy run and three snares would be enough. More than enough. Her hands built and laid the traps with the ease of long practice, and she finished just as the last glimmer of daylight drained out of the sky, leaving the mountain to strangle in a groggy dusk.

Back at the cottage, she found the old man asleep. In the darkness there was no sound at all but the breeze sifting through the eaves and the crackle of the soft rain against the glass, and then, after straining to catch it, the shallow, trickling whisper of breath. Beneath the pile of blankets, a small pile of skin and bones was putting up a frantic last stand. She watched for a while from the doorway, but there was little really to be seen.

Dawn broke late, given the rain. The girl left the house a little after six, and footing on the way down the mountain was difficult, especially in the darkness. But she found the snares easily.

The first of the three was empty, but the second held a medium-sized buck rabbit that would provide plenty of meat. He'd fought hard to get away and had eventually strangled himself in the snare, the wire cutting though the flesh of his throat almost to the bone. She wrestled him free and skinned and gutted him on the spot, tossing the waste and entrails into the long grass for the rats and crows to feast upon. Then she checked the third snare.

At first, she wasn't sure what she'd caught. The ground was badly rutted around the trap which indicated that the struggle to escape must have been immense. She gasped when she peeled back the torn mess of hair and flesh to identify a small tom cat. He must have wondered up here from the village in search of mice or small birds, or perhaps he was out looking for love. Either way, he'd picked the wrong night to stray.

It was then that the idea occurred to her. Without hesitating, she unfolded her grandfather's pocket knife and proceeded to skin the dead animal. After all, she thought, meat is meat. If the old man complained, she would tell him that all the snare had caught was a hare and that was probably why the food tasted a little off. Hares were a different kind of eating. Or she'd say that she used margarine in the frying because they were out of butter. She worked fast and ably, the blade of the knife carving through the brindled fur to peel the flesh away. The rats and crows would have one hell of a feast today, but it would be nothing compared to the treat her grandfather had in store. This wasn't like spitting in his food; this was a thousand times better.

Laughing from deep down in her chest, she separately packed the two parcels of meat, then started up the mountainside again.

THIS BIRD HAS FLOWN

This morning, I woke feeling very cold. A heavy drift of snow had fallen during the night, but the cloud cleared early and the temperatures must have plummeted. I looked out the window, but it was still a little dark to see very much. The glass was frosted over, in odd, vague swirls and clefts that made me think of stained glass windows in churches. Not the colours so much as the texture, that same hearty, chiselled effect that seemed to twist everything askew.

A memory hung over me, one from years before, dating back to the time I had gone to visit my aunt in hospital. Jenny, my father's sister. I must have been dreaming about her, though it didn't feel that way, and what I was remembering was what had happened, nothing particularly fantastic at all. She'd undergone an operation – for a woman's problem, I think; something painfully routine and permanent – but when I arrived at the hospital she was asleep, drunk on medication. Her bed was in the far right corner of a very bright six-bed ward, and I stood around for a minute or two just looking at her, thinking to myself how strange she looked, not really like her usual self at all. We had been so close growing up; she was twelve years older than me but we lived near one another and, as an only child, I had always looked upon her as a big sister. When I was eight or nine years old, I used to imagine that one day we'd marry, and of course I was too young then to understand that such a thing could never happen. I loved her that much, though, and I know she felt the same way about me. But then time played one of its deft tricks, and a day came when we were both more than a little shocked to realise that the ties had been undone and our lives had somehow grown apart.

That afternoon in the hospital, sleep, combined with the trauma of the surgery, had reduced her to a lump, and made a further stranger of her. Huddled under crisp white linen sheets, she looked old and overweight, a pulp of waxy flesh, dyed blonde corkscrew hair and brand new cerise pink silk pyjamas, and her face held a pointed expression, most probably because of the pain. Worry lines had slit faint ruts into her forehead with a determination that even the after-effects of an anaesthetic couldn't rub smooth, and her mouth constantly pursed and puckered, the lips pale without their daub of lipstick, as if she was speaking inside her dreams. When I was eight or nine, I'd been sure that one day our age gap would narrow enough so that it ceased to matter, but in actuality it had only seemed to widen.

I stood there, as I've said, for a minute or two, thinking that maybe it would be okay for me to just stoop and kiss her, a simple peck on her cheek or her brow and just for old times' sake, but a feeling of discomfort stirred and began to swell, eventually forcing me to turn away. The ward, because of its stillness and high ceilings, seemed to yawn emptily, and I had reached the door before I realised that a girl was watching me from the bed to my left. I smiled at her with some embarrassment, and I was about to push the door open when she smiled back. For some reason, that stopped me. There was something about her expression that seemed so forlorn I just couldn't bring myself to ignore it. I hesitated for an instant, then moved to the side of her bed. I glanced around for a visitor's chair, but found none, and she shuffled her body awkwardly and sat up in the bed, drawing up her legs in a way that made some room on the mattress and seemed to invite me to sit. I nodded, understanding, and perched on the edge of the bed; all very proper, but friendly too. The mattress was firm and didn't dip much beneath my weight. I had brought a small bunch of flowers for Jenny, nothing fancy, just some posies, and I held them out to this girl on impulse, sensing perhaps that she truly needed them.

'Well,' I said. 'The rain's stopped. The way it's been falling lately, I was beginning to think the government had stock in the stuff.'

Her face tensed with confusion, in a way that brought out the fully stupidity in my words.

'My name is Billy,' I added, and held my breath for a return.

Her name was Marketa. Her English, when it finally came, was soft and slow, fluent enough, but a long way from natural, withered in places and in others thickly over-pronounced, and she spoke with an uncertainty that echoed shyness as well as fear. I tried to make her feel at ease, and even though I could see that she was struggling with the hard corners of my accent, I rambled on and on, taking a shot at anything that came to mind, afraid for both our sakes of what the silence might bring if we let it take hold. She made sounds that I took to be agreeable, but the bemusement in her eyes spoke volumes. When I had fully exhausted the asinine and the small-talk became too much of a struggle, I skipped on into the safer, easier rut of asking questions, keeping a happy and upbeat voice and then nodding with exaggerated interest to her replies, leaning in to catch every nuance of her answers – as if they mattered at all one way or the other – and making sure to pull and bend my facial expressions to match their tone. She was forthright in everything she said, speaking as if from a textbook. We were playing a kind of game, one that she needed and one that I felt obliged to continue. None of it was easy. I gathered in the facts, made sympathetic gestures with my mouth and tried my best to make her feel important, at least for a little while.

She had left her home, she said, a small town called Stonava, in the Czech Republic's eastern region, to make a new life with her boyfriend. They had tried Paris first, but Paris was a hard city, unwelcoming, and after a couple of months they decided to give Ireland a go. That had been a little over a year before. She liked Cork, she said, but there was something in her smile that seemed to add a caveat to that, and she saw me notice and shrugged. It could be lonely at times, she added, not really needing to make mention of the boyfriend again, because that was a well-worn tale of woe.

A week ago, she had been to see a doctor, for something to ease the pain that crept up and down her side and which seemed to be getting increasingly worse. He took some blood, and the following day phoned her to come in for further tests. Only a week, a little less than that, even, but already the bed had made a mess of her, just as it had with Jenny. I lowered my gaze as she talked and, without meaning to, took to studying her hands. They were delicate hands, pale skinned and demure, the bones spraying out from her wrists and rising in spindles to the jut of her knuckles. Her fingers were slender, with meticulously trimmed nails, and she were no rings, not even the mark of one. She'd been chasing promises. Her voice kept on and on, just a little above a hush and delectably foreign, the vowels of her words carrying all the throaty allure of a Cold War spy film. I watched as she folded and resettled her hands over and over, gently wrestling in and out of a prayerful grip and occasionally worrying the hem of the bed's pale blue woollen blanket. I didn't realise she was even crying until I looked up again.

'Since the doctor told me, I've been thinking about home. But I can't go back. That would be too sad.'

What was there to say? I didn't know this girl at all. I had her name, as well as an image burnt into my mind, but nothing else. I felt something shift inside of me, but I put that down to pity, and I had a notion that it wasn't right to feel that way. Her hands parted, fluttered uncertainly or dismissively in the air and then slumped down to lie in her lap, fingers of her left hand overlapping at a slant the fingers of the right. I wanted to say something, to offer some few words of solace, but nothing came to mind.

'I don't sleep now,' she added, in a whisper. A tear chased a runnel down one cheek and clung to the ridge of her jaw. In the strong white light I could clearly see the trace it left behind. More tears bristled in her eyes and I remember thinking that they blurred vision in the very same way as stained glass. Not the colour, of course, but that texture. When you give the matter some thought, you realise that it takes very little to contort the world; one tear can ruin everything if it has a good reason to fall. I took a handkerchief from my pocket, reached out and dried her eyes. It was a reflex gesture; she'd become a child, and without tensing she surrendered wholly to it. 'When I do drift off,' she said, 'terrible things are waiting. I'm not so troubled about what happens to me in the dreams as I am about how it affects the people around me. Even strangers cry for me, and I don't want that. At least, I don't think I do.'

After a little while, a bell went off somewhere, and a few minutes after that a nurse came to the door and said that she was very sorry, but visiting hours were over. I nodded and stood. The girl in the bed, Marketa, looked up at me. She thanked me for talking to her and also for the flowers, and neither of us mentioned the fact that both occurrences had been accidents, twists of fate. Unsure what to say, I leaned down and kissed her cheek, which made her blush but also smile with something like happiness. She dealt with that smile by chewing on one side of her lower lip, but I saw past that and was glad that I'd done it. I mumbled a so long, and assured her that I'd call again, that I had to come back anyway because my aunt, Jenny, down there in the last bed across, had slept right through my visit. Jenny could hold onto a grudge until a day after forever, I said, though that was nearly the very opposite of true. I almost smiled as I watched the girl's expression grow bemused again.

That was it. We mean a lot of the things we say, and I fully intended to go back, but life, work and a dozen other excuses conspired to keep me grounded. Then Jenny was discharged, armed with a crutch and a distant stare. We spoke on the phone as often as I was around to answer and, when she began to feel a little better, we made coffee dates to fill up Saturday mornings and picked at pecan and maple syrup muffins while she rambled on about hospital food and I chugged my eyebrows over cheesy, Groucho-styled double entendre cracks about wanting to see her scar.

'The girl?' she said, and smirked while I plucked at her for information. 'Oh yeah. I recognised your handiwork there, all right. A kid in floods of tears and a vase of wilting posies. Also, the nurse mentioned you were by. So thanks, I suppose. But you still owe me a bunch of flowers, okay? And nothing that you've lifted out of a graveyard, if you don't mind.'

Floods of tears. I recalled how, after leaving the hospital, I had spent a good part of the bus ride home trying to tag her with an age. My best guess put her somewhere in her mid-twenties, though it wouldn't have surprised me if the truth lay some five years either side of that. Funny how five years can be the world at that age, or it can be nothing. Depends, I suppose, on the person. And funny, but not in a good way. She hadn't been an awful lot to look at, but I put most of that down to the collateral damage of her treatment, and even if her skin was rough and blotched and her hair spun around her face in lank, tawny tendrils, there was no denying that she still had nice eyes, large, just the way I like them, and a shade of green so pale that in lesser light they had probably often passed for grey. Or silver. Her tears had made them glisten, and made everything seem fleeting, delicately poised but waiting to be torn asunder.

Using my thumbnail to scrape muffin residue from the channels of the pleated paper cup, I pretended that my interest in Marketa was one of simple curiosity. Which, I suppose, it was. Still, it had all the feel of an act, and Jenny's smirk cut newer, deeper divots into the flesh of her upper lip, ending finally in the revelation of teeth.

'They moved her out of the ward a couple of days before I was allowed home. She didn't talk much, but I think she'd been given some pretty bad news. The doctors seemed very interested in her, and that's never a good thing.' My aunt broke her second muffin into chunks and picked out the pecans to eat first. I watched her, wishing she could have told me more.

This morning, the scree of frost combined with the tempered darkness to make something ethereal of the early hour. Beyond the window, snow lay banked along the ditches and hedgerows, its bleak pallor adding depth to the silence. It felt like weather for dying.

Hospitals have this way of emphasising the strangeness between people. The setup almost craves vulnerability and, with its cloying antiseptic stench, overly waxed floors and stultifying artificial glow, it quickly peels away whatever modicum of familiarity we might hold dear, until patients are reduced down to mush and visitors to hollow, creaking shells. This is a reality of our world. Perhaps though, it is because of this that we are allowed to hit upon some common note, a kind of knowing camaraderie, like survivors of some terrible disaster, or war veterans. I sometimes think that it is for just such reasons that we dream. At a time when social evolution threatens to send us spinning into space, scientists still scratch their heads in wonder at this most archaic of habits. They see dreaming as an obtuse reflex, some primeval semaphore worthless in our new world and lingering only for nostalgia's sake. But dreams store up all the memories, hopes and fears that in our daily lives we overcome or simply toss away, and I think we need constant reminders of those things in order to balance and counteract the way that we have chosen to live today.

I peeled off my T-shirt and dressed quickly, foregoing the notion of a shower. That was okay; today was my own, and I had no place to be, nothing much at all to do. I was clean enough for just milling around the house. The cold bit at me, savage teeth nuzzling my skin, but I've known colder mornings. 'Marketa,' I whispered, because there was no one around to hear. I think I was hoping that by speaking of my dream, I'd somehow clear it from my mind, but the sound of it, my crushed voice, made me flinch. It seemed ripe with accusation. I paused, then I repeated the name, this time in my usual speaking voice. But that felt no better.

It was far too early to be getting up, but the day yawned all around me, its needs waiting to be filled, and I've never been one of those people who can just lie around once they've woken. Today was Sunday, an open-book kind of day and one simply built for idling. But there were right ways to idle. I decided that a walk would probably do me some good; take in some fresh air, wrapped up tight and warm against the cold. The exercise would help to build an appetite. Then, after a hearty breakfast, I could settle down with the papers and listen to a bit of *Rubber Soul*. Full of the feeling that I had wandered headlong into the early act of a story without an end, I sat on the edge of my bed and laced up my boots.

BETTER DAYS

It wasn't so surprising, I suppose, that I should have failed to recognise her. Fourteen years had passed and a lot of toll had been taken. Life, some people call it; the daily grind of growing up and taking on the scars and nests of wrinkles that come with raising kids, trying to mine a lively ore from the stupor of a teaching post, secretarial work or something yet more manual and muscle-aching, saving hard – basically doing whatever it takes to ensure survival. People change like the wind, outside as well as in.

That afternoon, I found myself on a street in a relatively far-away town, attending to some inoffensive manner of business and trying to spend some of the spare minutes until my appointment doing a spot of window-shopping, when, without the least bit of warning, the heavens opened. Not just rain, either, but a deluge. The sky convulsed and the rain fell in great heaves, the low gloom spouted flames of lightning, and thunder clapped and rippled overhead, the angriest sound in the whole world short of a bitter wife scolding a long-whipped husband.

In a mass of panic, people began to run for cover, barging their way into every available shadowy recess or gaping doorway. I ran too, blind to direction, all notions of logic pumping from my mind with every flailing gasp of drenched air. All along the way, bodies huddled against shop-front windows while candy-striped canopies and awnings strained and sagged above their bowed heads in a valiant effort to protect them from the worst edges of the onslaught. I blundered past these walls of terrified faces, up along the street, my own fear as thick as a second apple in my throat, my feet battering something jazzy out of the pavement.

It must have been mere seconds, surely no more than a minute at the most, but the weather's beating was so intense and brutal that I had just about surrendered to my fate when sanctuary revealed itself, in the form of an already occupied telephone box. A door wrestled partially open just as I was about to pass, a God-given chasm barely enough to reveal a beckoning hand of mercy. Without thought or consideration, I plunged inside.

'Thank you,' I gasped, just as soon as I could catch a swallow of breath, and I felt myself nodding a few times, as if the gesture could add something in the way of gratitude that no mere words could hope to approach.

The owner of that helping hand, a woman of somewhere around my own age, did something with her mouth, a certain leftward dragging of her lips that seemed to resonate with the oddest sense of familiarity, but then she turned her dishevelled gaze out through the scratched plastic-glass walls to the traumatised day beyond and whatever had stirred awake in my mind or in my heart drifted back into its slumber again.

'It's like the end of the world out there,' she said, just as a sodden sheet of newspaper wrapped itself hard against the angle of the box. Instinctively, I squinted to read the headline, something about a triumphant piece of deconstructive surgery on a set of conjoined twins, the swapping of organs and eyes and that sort of thing, a genuine honest-to-goodness miracle, but before I could gather in any sort of really worthwhile details, a cross-wind hit and dragged the sheet free to go flapping and tumbling on down the street.

She glanced at me after a moment had passed. 'You okay now?'

'Yeah, I guess so.' I tried on a smile that wrinkled the bridge of my nose, and shrugged. 'That'll teach me to go out without checking on the weather forecast,' I added, words that felt and tasted stupid as they lay jumbled in my throat, but which sounded ten or a hundred times worse once they had jarred themselves free into actual sound. Wind howled at our backs and all around us, buffeting the phone box in a truly bullying way. 'Thanks again for letting me in,' I said. 'If you hadn't I'd very likely be on my way to Oz right now.'

'It's fine,' she said, and reached up to pull a rope of tawny fringe from her eyes. There wasn't room for so much as a handkerchief between us, hardly the situation to find yourself in with a stranger, unless that stranger happens to be a beautiful woman, yet even in this confined space she managed to study me up and down. That rolling stare felt familiar too, its detached consideration swinging between clemency and judgement, and I tried my best not to flinch, not to yield too much detail so early on in the game.

'You're soaked right through.'

Her large witch-hazel eyes glistened with a magical intensity, set to heightened life by her own harried encounter with the storm, and perhaps too by finding my stranger's body in such close and sudden proximity with her own. After a veritable black hole of a pause her mouth shifted again, restless with more to say.

Trying to help, I refreshed my smile, that same pinchnosed smirk that, even with the hindrance of a lazily sprouting beard, had this way of making a fourteen-year-old boy out of my face.

'I'm sorry,' she said, after a silence began to pool between us. 'It's just, well, do I know you? I mean to say, you look familiar to me. At least, I think you do. You're not a teacher at my son's school, are you? I know it's silly, but there's something …'

'I'm Billy,' I said, and had a go at raising and offering my hand. The result wasn't a triumph, but she recognised the effort at least and played along. We grasped hands with some awkward flexing of wrists.

'Rebecca.'

And that, for me anyway, was the key to the door.

'Rebecca,' I said, putting on a thoughtful act. 'I knew a Rebecca once.' She deserved the chance to catch up; it felt like the very least I could do, in the circumstances. 'Except she was a Becky then, not a Rebecca.' I shrugged my shoulders again, even though the slightest movement had consequences here in the confines of this box. 'Well, that was a long time ago. In Douglas. And I suppose she would have outgrown the Becky sooner or later. I mean, we all have to grow up, don't we?'

All that witch-hazel blazed, and I was overcome with details of such intensity that I just had to wonder how they could ever have been forgotten. Golden summer times spent climbing trees, building bonfires, tossing a ball around and catching frogs; then, later on, holding hands and learning the rules of different games.

'In Douglas? Oh my God, I don't believe it. Not Billy … It is, isn't it? Billy, from …'

I smiled again, while all around us the veils of time just slipped away. She looked the same, I realised now. The skin around her eyes was a little more stretched, her hair was done differently and her mouth had lost some of its younger ease, but those were minor alterations. With very little effort I could see her as she used to be: bossy, sharp as a wasp's peck, and lovely. None of this made sense, of course, but I had grown used to that a long time ago.

For the next ten minutes or so we were twelve or thirteen again, had pitched back in time to balance once more on that tricky cusp where things said in jest carried serious implications quite often far into the future, where the need to know everything about everything and everyone felt as critical as breathing or learning off the latest chart-topping hit, and where tomorrow seemed years off in the misty distance and the age of some such ridiculous number as twenty or, God forbid, thirty was too mind-blowing to even contemplate.

By mutual consent, the formalities were bypassed, the questions about parents and siblings, that sort of thing. 'I've read some of your work,' she said, her tone a coin toss really between disparaging and complimentary, but most likely neither, just a typical echo of the pragmatism I so well remembered now. I smiled, but ventured no further down that road; not wanting to have my feelings hurt, I didn't press the subject. It was enough, I suppose, to know that she was aware of me, that I had crossed her mind at least occasionally in all the years since we'd been apart. I enquired about her own lot in life, not trying to probe, honestly wanting the answer to be somewhere in the affirmative. She was a housewife, she said, daring me to respond. Her husband was an accountant with a well-known firm here in town, had just recently, in fact, stepped up into a senior position. He was older than her – 'by a few years' was how she put it – but they were really quite deliriously happy. Life had found a good shape for her, granted her all manner of precious gifts.

Together, she and Zachary – Zachary being Mr Perfectly Right – had been blessed with two beautiful children, a boy, Raymond, and a girl, Elisabeth, a nice house in the suburbs and two cars. All in all, she had lucked into an exceedingly comfortable existence. So, yes, she had carved out a wonderful life for herself. I wanted to ask about her medical ambitions, at exactly which point along the teenage road did dreams of surgical greatness begin to dissipate and, also, why she and the clearly wonderful Zach had chosen such full and cumbersome names for such young children, but I wasn't certain that our time apart could be scaled so easily as to allow me such ease with the facts of her current and recent world, and I certainly didn't want to start a fight, at least not while we were standing almost toe to toe in a telephone box.

'Are you married?' she said.

I had noticed her checking out my hand for signs of a ring, but of course not every married man wore a wedding ring. I shook my head, not quite sure why I was even considering telling a lie. On a page, I can lie with the very best of them, but that's because no one has to watch my lips move. And Becky had always had a natural radar when it came to my tall tales and excuses. Don't ever try taking me for a fool, she used to say, stating the patently obvious. I didn't doubt that Rebecca would have inherited a lot, if not all, of Becky's hard-earned talents.

'No,' I said, trying to make nothing out of the fact. 'So far, I've been able to dodge that particular fastball.'

'Well, is there someone special?' I remembered her as one of those children who could never let a cut just heal. Her nails were forever picking at a scab, as if in the flow or trickle of blood there could be wondrous secrets to behold. Her picking hand had crept up into view now; she held it crooked between her chest and mine, and when she spoke, her fingers shifted and flittered, seemingly of their own accord, but almost as if they were directing the words.

I looked into her eyes and recalled games played back in overgrown fields, games of chase, of hide and seek and, as time went by and her curiosity became catching, contests of truth or dare.

'No,' I replied, knowing that it was what she wanted to hear, whatever her reasons. 'No one special. Not for a long time.'

The rain outside the box began to sag and, rather too quickly, abate. The breeze held sway a little longer, and the glass walls around us continued to groan against the strain. Thunder rolled, but with less vehemence than before, and I knew that the storm had already put miles between itself and this street. Occasional streaks of lightning continued to flicker glare into the afternoon, though hardly more now than spastic twinkles, little obligatory reflexes of light. Our time was up all over again; people were already peeling themselves from their places of shelter, and now was the time to pick up the dropped treads of our lives, such as they had become. In another few minutes, our situation, a man and a woman pinned together into a telephone box built for one, strangers or, worse still, age-old friends, would rightfully cause eyebrows to start twitching skywards.

'Listen, Becky, I mean Rebecca,' I said, deciding to make things easy for her, whether or not easy was what was required. 'I've got an appointment that I really should try to keep. But this has meant the world to me, running into you like this, really, it has. Here,' I added, just as the phone-box door's accordion hinges bent into action and spilled me out onto the street. I went into an inside pocket, found a pen and a small notebook and scribbled down a number and, after a moment of pause, an address too. She took the piece of paper I held out, read it in her old meticulous way then folded it into perfect quarters, or at least as close to perfection as could be achieved on a page with a perforated fringe, and tucked it into her purse.

'Thanks,' she said, promising nothing. A little thaw was probably too much to have hoped for, but I was still disappointed.

'I wish to God we had more time,' I said, meaning that with all my heart. 'There's so much I'd like to ask you, and it would be great to go back over old times.' A smile was probably pushing the boat out beyond its safe depth, but I'm not the worst swimmer in the world. 'We had some good ones, didn't we?'

'We were kids,' she said, her words dismissive but not unyielding, and she did that thing with her mouth again. I watched, feeling like the gesture was for my benefit, that old Zachary didn't get nearly the same feeling of warmth from that tiny tugging. Most likely, he wouldn't even have noticed it, just as he probably missed the way she liked to touch the little silver hoop in her earlobe whenever she listened to a song she liked or how she had always tried to deny a fancy for a particularly vibrant shade of the colour red. Or maybe I had him wrong, maybe his accountant's hawkish eyes logged everything, and understood them, treasured them for what they were, his wife's beautiful foibles.

I nodded and held out a hand. She took it, her fingers as cool and delicate as I remembered, and delicious in my grip. I did my best not to hold on too tight, but she winced anyway, ever so slightly. Perhaps that had become a reflex reaction for her. 'Well, Rebecca,' I said. Then, with a smile, I nodded goodbye.

'Wait,' she said, with enough urgency of tone to make her blush.

I stood there, half-turned.

'I have your number,' she said, 'and I promise to call. But you know how it is, Bill. With the best intentions in the world, things happen. We get locked into other tasks and plans get delayed, a week or two, then a month. Then, before you know where you are, another fourteen years have rumbled by. You start covering up the first grey hairs and counting the wrinkles, and soon enough you've run clean out of time.'

She smiled, but it bent sadly at the corners, and it took every single ounce of my hardly legendary willpower not to sweep her up into my arms and to speckle her face with kisses.

'So,' she continued, after a pause, 'let's both accept that I really do intend to call. It would, after all be nice to go back home, if only to show the children where their mother came from, and to see how much the old place has changed. We could catch up, I could introduce you to my family, we could tell stories and embarrass one another to within an inch of exploding. But let's also accept and understand that it may not actually happen, okay? And if this should be the case, I think it's best that we prepare ourselves. If I'm wrong, great, but let's both assume that this will be the very last time we ever see or speak to one another.'

'Which makes this goodbye the real thing, is that it?'

'Who knows,' she said, whispered. 'But maybe.'

I nodded.

'The thing is, Bill, assuming the worst, I think that if there is one thing, anything at all, that you regret not saying to me back when we were kids, why not go ahead and mention it? Or if you have a question that you'd like answered, I promise that I'll be as truthful and upfront as I possibly can.'

It was just like her, to be the bigger person. She scraped back that frond of hair from her brow again and tucked it back into her clip-held fringe, her eyes fixed on mine. I looked for love, or even some hint of affection, but if some such feeling did truly exist still, it was so well tucked away among the more determined details that recognition proved on the difficult side of impossible. Practical to the last, she wanted loose ends bound so that they might be more easily forgotten.

I pretended to consider her offer, though the important questions had already formed an orderly queue in my mind. Why she had broken up our friendship? Did she ever regret the way she had treated me, dropping me like a stone the first time someone more exciting showed her the least bit of interest? Were there ever moments when she found herself longing for the better times we shared, back when I'd make up the most ridiculous stories just to make her laugh, or did she ever take a minute out of her day or night to imagine how differently her life might have turned out had we continued with our romance? And lastly, I suppose, did she ever look for or recognise herself among the casually coded pages of stories and novels that I have written?

The answers to any of these questions would have satisfied an ancient but still wickedly irritating itch, and I felt myself tottering on the edge of such a lucky dip, but just as I was about to speak, something deep inside caused me to hold my breath.

She gazed up at me, expectation rich on her pretty lips.

'I can't think of a single thing,' I said at last. 'You were right, Rebecca. We were just kids, and it all seems so long ago.' I smiled, and it felt like a release, like I had kicked my way out of a stifling second skin. 'But it's been lovely to see you again after all these years. You look as good as I remember, and I'm happy that your life has turned out so well.' Then, without giving her time to rebuke or encourage anything more, I leaned in and kissed the corner of her mouth.

'Goodbye,' I whispered, then turned away.

An hour later, I sat in a fourth-floor waiting room, still with fifteen minutes to spare before my appointment. The storm had well and truly drummed itself dry, and late-afternoon sunlight seeped through the window and fell in a golden spill across part of the floor. To pass the remaining time and just for something to distract me from my thoughts, my fingers rubbed their way through the clammy pages of an old issue of the *National Geographic*. With the greatest of effort, I trawled the words and glossy photographs of articles about a revitalised Sarajevo, the courage of a solo round-the-world yachtswoman and some scientific wishful thinking as to the possibilities of micro-organic life existing on Jupiter's third and largest moon, Ganymede, but all the offered facts skipped through my mind and away, and finally I gave up on my reading and dropped the magazine back onto the coffee table. Then, for just a minute, I leaned back in my chair, closed my eyes and let in thoughts of who I was and of who I had become. Amid jumbled notions of missed opportunities, lucky escapes and a surely infinite clutter of alternate realities, I sighed happily.

THE BLACK AND TAN

Everything had happened so fast, and when Cavendish tried to make sense of it all the details just swam together, a mass of confusion.

His battalion had been marching since eight or so that morning, but even though the day had turned the corner of noon, their destination, Castletown, still lay miles away. The men had settled into the routine of mindless walking, fourteen of them drifting along behind the Lieutenant's slow-moving car and holding their rifles slung across their shoulders or cradled in their arms.

The ambush hit along a twisting stretch of road that left them helpless to fight back, a broad hairpin bend that leaned into high ground with the perfect cover of woodland sweeping down from the right and the land falling away steeply into the valley on the left. A shot rang out, squealing against the metal of the car, and then several more shots were fired in such quick succession that there was nothing for the soldiers to do but hunch low and try desperately to crack off return shots of their own.

A few had run, and he had been one of those.

Now, the muddy sky heaved and gave up its first cold drops of rain. Within a minute or two it overcame its initial hesitation and became the downpour that had threatened since dawn, but even the weight of that was not enough to mute the occasional bark of gunfire off in the distance.

His lungs hurt from running. When he finally stopped, he'd made perhaps two miles, and he bent over at the waist and checked the chambers of his pistol while he tried to catch his breath. Knowing already that the gun had been fired empty, but hoping, nonetheless. He holstered the weapon, buttoned the flap closed, and looked around. Christ. This part of Ireland was nothing but fields. Two miles and he was no closer to anything.

Then he saw them, the men, six of them, stretched out in a line along the land's southern incline and starting down through the fields towards him. He had nothing but an empty gun, and there was nowhere to run. With a sigh of resignation, he watched them close in; well, there had to be a loser in every battle.

'Right,' one of them said. 'We'll have that gun.' He looked very young, too young for all of this, not more than fifteen or sixteen. But that was the kind of war this was, and age had nothing to do with it. This one's narrow, drooping frame made him seem taller than he probably was, but he held a rifle low and looked comfortable enough with it, like he knew how to use it, and his voice had a detached ease that made it through what should have been an otherwise smothering sing-song brogue.

Cavendish watched the rest of the men move in and

then spread out around him in a loose arc, then he nodded and slowly drew the pistol, careful to hold it only with his fingertips, and tossed it onto the ground. Its barrel speared in the soft tilled earth of the field, but that didn't matter.

'It's empty anyway,' he said, raising his hands up and away from his body. The rain was coming down hard now, and he stopped holding himself against it and just gave in. The men were ten feet back and the line they held was to give him a chance to run, if he was of a mind to make this easy for everyone.

The one who had already spoken seemed in charge, even though there were men in this group who had to be forty if they were a day. They watched him for their lead and he instructed mostly in gestures. A shift of his head, just the smallest movement, and one of the men stepped forward for the gun, checked it and pushed it inside the waistband of his trousers. A glance, and another of the men moved in behind Cavendish, dragged his arms down from their spread and bound them at the wrists with a hard, fibrous twine that quickly bit into the flesh.

'I'm Reilly,' the young man said, though there was no need for introductions or explanations. 'Commander of the Rathgannon column.' He glanced back over his shoulder. 'In case you're wondering, you're the last. The rest are dead. We got most of them on the road. It was easy enough running down the rest.'

Cavendish stared at him, giving away nothing, even though all was already lost.

When he was tied securely, they began to walk, down across this field and the next, down to where the valley flattened out. There was the sound of a stream, the unmistakable beat of fast-running water even through the percussive shuffle of the rain, but there was nothing to be seen, not yet. Only fields, muted shades of green running one into the next.

The men kept Cavendish ten or twelve paces ahead of them, but no one spoke any more. There was something comforting now about the rain, how it fattened the air, its coldness making everything feel clean. When they reached a low river they didn't even slow, simply waded out into it and across. The far bank was slippery and they had to struggle on hands and knees to climb it, and as Cavendish was first he knew there was a moment when he could have tried running. But he didn't, just stood there until the others were on their feet. One of them said, 'That way,' and pushed him on, but gently. Everything had already been decided, of course, and in a strange way they no longer felt like enemies, even though their rifles were never far from his back.

After about twenty minutes they reached a copse of elms. The rush of another unseen stream beat noise into the day, its urgency agitating and unsettling. Reilly raised a hand, and some of the men fanned out to ensure that the place was secure. A formality, but it was attention to even the most trifling of details that ensured survival. Not strength, not even courage. 'What are you?' he asked. 'Scottish?'

Cavendish nodded and said that, yes, he was from a place called Dumbarton, not far from Glasgow.

'What in Christ's name brought you over here?'

There was no answer to that, none that would have made

a difference. A wife and family who needed food, no work anywhere.

'Well,' Reilly said, as if it was out of his hands now, not really his decision at all. 'You've made your choice, Tan. If you have a prayer that you want to say, now would be the time.' Cavendish looked at the young man for a moment, then lowered his eyes and shook his head gently. He'd long since fallen out of the habit of praying. And anyway, how would God hear him out here?

Two men had moved behind him, and they took him by the arms and shoulders, led him to a spread of open ground and urged him to his knees. He went without a struggle. The ground was muddy and moss-ridden; the coarse wool of his trousers drew in the moisture like a sponge. It crossed his mind that his body might never be found, not out here, not for months or even years. Some day a man out hunting for rabbits or pheasant would happen across his bones, and maybe he'd report his find or maybe he'd just hurry away, not wanting to get involved.

'I have a letter,' he said, looking up. A white light poked through the tangled branches, causing him to wince. He hoped that they wouldn't think it was because he was afraid. He'd spent two years in the trenches, had survived first Verdun and then Passchendaele. Now he was going to die, alone and unknown, slumped on his knees in some god-forsaken bog-end of a field in Ireland. 'Here. In my breast pocket. It's to my wife. Could you see that it gets sent?'

Someone off in the trees snorted softly, a contemptuous sound, but then Reilly stepped forward, unbuttoned the pocket and removed the letter. His young face grew hard and strained, many times its own age, as he stared for a second or two at the envelope, maybe reading the scrawled name and address through the myriad creases and sweat stains, maybe just trying to feel some hint of another man's life. Then he slipped the letter into his own pocket. Cavendish gazed up at him, waiting for the assurance of a nod or a positive word, but none was forthcoming, and at last the light's glare forced the captured soldier to look away.

'Close your eyes, if you like,' Reilly said, and Cavendish, head still slung low, nodded and tried. But the darkness spun time into something terribly unwholesome, and every breath was made unbearable by the idea that it might be the last. There was nothing much to see, just a gleaming pond of grey mud and an array of filthy, clotted boots, some with the leather worn so thin across the toes that hints of their steel caps showed through. He heard a click as a pistol was armed very close to his left ear, and he pinched his lips tightly together and swallowed hard.

The first shot put him down, and was probably enough, but Reilly turned the body over with his foot and lowered the muzzle of his own pistol right against one staring eye before firing off a second shot. Some of the other men turned their heads away and looked very pale, because killing was not yet a taste that they could bear with comfort. Reilly made a scraping sound in his throat and spit into the mud beside the body as if trying to rid his mouth of just such a taste, but actually it was a gesture for the others, because if they were going to win their war they'd need many more days like this, and they'd need to see this as a success rather than an atrocity. 'Fucking Black an' Tan,' he hissed, then stalked off into the trees, to say a prayer and to be sick.

ON THE BEACH

Out on the beach, this late in the evening, there were only two shades to the whole world, the brazen yellow of fading light and the blackened press of shadows. Jack had said goodbye to everyone in the village, had already locked up his home and handed over the key to the new owners. By this time tomorrow he'd have put down the first day of a meticulously laid-out future, but standing here, basking in the last hour of his old life and with the dark sea spread out before him, the stillness as immense as the sky above, it was impossible to believe that any place as hectic and demanding as London could even exist. Tomorrow, he'd be a part of that other world, tomorrow and all the days after, for the rest of his life. A world made better by Cassandra, but still, a world that would feel strange to him.

The tide was coming in, but slowly. Low waves broke hushed against the beach, the short dogleg of shoreline penned in by cliffs and the sand shone just a shade deeper than the small wintertime wedge of moon. He hugged his arms against the cold of the coming night, watched the stars sparking into view off to the east, pinhead sharp and emerging through the darkness, and decided that there would be a stiff frost by dawn, enough to whiten the fields. But by dawn he'd be one of a crowd, bustling through an airport and then a tube station, choking back his uncertainty and trying with all his might to smile. He walked slowly just inside the high water line, feeling the sand firm beneath his heels. There were so many reasons to go, he told himself, and none, really, to stay. London would be a well-spring of excitement. A new job was already waiting, a position as copy-editor for a tabloid newspaper that might not be the most inspiring in the world, not yet anyway, but which at least put him close to the cutting edge and would surely lead on to bigger, brighter things. He'd have a foot in the door, and from there, well, who knew what might happen. And of course, London had Cassandra, his true reason for going, if the truth be told.

He knew by the way she looked at him that she loved him, and wasn't that enough to qualify him as the luckiest man in the world? Her face came easily to his mind, the settling night a help now, a blank canvas just waiting to be filled. With pale, unblemished skin, deep almond-shaped, hazel-coloured eyes and sleek elongated features, she was beautiful and gentle, and when they were together he always felt as though the rest of the world just ceased to exist, or to matter. Once, out for dinner, they had sat staring into one another's eyes for a solid hour, not speaking, hardly more than smiling, and they'd been so entranced that they'd forgotten even to eat. Finally the maître d' had wandered over and discreetly cleared his throat, but he was an elderly man who had seen everything there was to see in a restaurant, and he leaned in and suggested, not unkindly, that it would save them both a good deal of money to do their stargazing elsewhere. 'Sir is a lucky man,' he had uttered, in that tone used for imparting secrets, after Cassandra had excused herself to powder her nose. That was a London thing, too; nobody around here ever powdered their nose. Perhaps it was the sea air that made such a chore unnecessary. Jack had listened, considered those words, then nodded agreement to the maître d', but a part of him couldn't help but feel detached. He was fulfilling a duty, he supposed, living up to what was expected of him. It was civilised behaviour to date a beautiful woman, to take her out for meals or to the theatre, perfectly in fitting with the new life that he was building for himself, far away from the shore. And he was very fond of Cassandra. Every time her mouth curved with happiness, his heartbeat raced a marathon. That had to count for something, and was probably more than a lot of people had, but love was such a big word.

People take so much for granted, he decided. Like walking on a beach in the darkness. This was utter solitude; even the scant sounds of the town couldn't make it to the water's edge. Out here, he might have been the last man on earth. Well, he often felt that way. It was lonely, sometimes, but not really so bad. The waves broke softly, chasing a pale frothy fringe up across the sand to within a few yards of where he walked, and he kept an idle pace, just savouring the relentless ease of the sound, the gentle conversation between the sea and the land. The darkness of the hour thickened, making him tremble. He tried to wish that Cassandra could have been here with him, that they could be walking hand in hand, sharing whispers and kisses and whatever was special about this moment. But it wasn't an honest wish. Perhaps to torture himself, he tried to picture her smile, but the effort was half-hearted. Another image stormed his mind instead, one that he had been avoiding ever since he'd made his decision to move to London. A memory, of a night not unlike this one, but years ago, ten at least, though it seemed longer, centuries ago. A night spent right here on the beach, but not spent alone.

He and Katie were far too young to know what love was. Everyone said that, all the adults who acted as if they were authorities on everything, and they spoke seriously, the amusement evident only in the gleam of their eyes. 'Have a good time,' his own father had told him, 'but don't be a fool about it.' Jack didn't think anyone could help being a fool though, not where someone like Katie was concerned. She wasn't beautiful, not in the conventional meaning of the word; she had a hard-boned, almost masculine, face and skin that suffered with the seasons, she wore her hair long and massively unkempt and battled constantly with her weight. But the person she was far outshone the negatives, until they meant nothing. Maybe the adults were right, maybe they were too young to understand what love was, but all he knew was that when she spoke to him he lit up like an inferno and whenever he thought about her he felt as though he'd been lifted up to the sky. If it wasn't love, he decided, it would surely do until love came along.

The moon blazed, small and bleak, a spun conch shape bleached to bone. He stared at it as he strolled, wondering what it knew. Only part of the face was visible, a war-damaged sliver of a face, but he felt the one eye's stare. The moon saw everything and everyone, he supposed, even as it dragged the water like a blanket up over the beach. Back then it had stared down on him and Katie.

'When we have kids,' she said, 'we'll take them walking here every night.'

'Kids? Slow down a bit, Mother Jones. There are some things to do before the kids come along, you know.' He was smiling, but the silence spun out and dredged up the unspoken things in his words. Katie was walking close beside him, her fingers interlaced with his. In her free hand she carried her sandals. She hated to get sand into her shoes, said that once the grains got in there they could never be made to leave. To help ease the silence of its burden, she glanced at him, held his eyes a moment and smiled, showing pretty teeth.

'Come on,' she said. 'Let's go for a swim.'

'What? Christ, Katie, it's the middle of winter.'

'It's March,' she said. 'That's practically summer.'

'Well, still, I'll bet the water's freezing. And what if someone sees us?'

'So what if they do?' Her smile widened, then seemed to shiver away. Gently, she pulled her hand from his; with reluctance, he let her, and just stood watching, not moving, while she unbuttoned her coat and then wrestled free of her heavy wool sweater. In less than a minute she was naked, the first time he had seen her so. She stood there, her shoulders hunched and vulnerable, her eyes demurely lowered, and the moonlight bathed her body in that pale, ethereal glow of miraculous things. The details of her flesh were just as he had often imagined, stocky yet fragile, porcelain yet grainy, a young bundle of contradictions; yet he seemed to sense that there was something different about her too, something more than his mind could ever have guessed. Perhaps he'd been sensing some danger.

When her vulnerability grew too intense, she turned and ran into the tide, shrieking wild, terrified laughter with every wading step. Jack watched, but hesitated in following. He felt nervous about the cold and about everything that the night entailed. But the running and receding tide-line dared him across, and he was sixteen years old, and the sea and Katie would only wait so long.

They met waist-deep, a flailing embrace that knocked them off-balance and drew them further out. He went under, flushed with panic, then resurfaced and thrilled to the whole world in his arms. The searing cold made breathing difficult, and what followed was a dizzying dream of laughter, flesh, lapping waves and shifting sands. And then suddenly she was gone.

He shuddered at the memory, and hunched deep into the comfort of his overcoat. Tomorrow, he'd be in London. He stooped to pick up a stone, a palm-sized piece of quartz made smooth by centuries of waves. The water had pressed and flattened, but it was time that carried the real weight, he knew, time that changed the face of everything. Even in the darkness, he could make out little white veins across the stone's surface, crisscrossing lifelines. He heaved it as far as he could out into the water, then waited too long before realising that the sound of the splash was probably too small to catch.

People knew at a glance that he had not been to blame. Even Katie's father had come to him, later, and in a small voice said that sometimes things just happened. That the world was not perfect and that God, if there was such a person or a thing, had a lot to answer for. Those must have been difficult words to say.

At the end of the beach, he stopped. The rocks rose up deep against the night, poking black reefs that led out to the headland. The sand beneath his feet was still fine, but a lot of kelp had gathered just here and the cold still air carried a cloying tinge of iodine. He knew that it was almost time to leave. He had already cried his fill over Katie, had already said goodbye a hundred times. Swallowing gulps of air in an effort to remove the ache from his throat, tasting the iodine on his tongue and on his lips, he turned at last from the sea and started up the foot-worn path towards and through the dunes above. But as he neared the top he froze. A breeze had started up from somewhere, just enough to carry some sound past his ear before dying away, and it had all the sense of a whispered word. He turned slowly, afraid of what he might see, but there appeared to be nothing out of the ordinary, just the pale dogleg of the sand, and the sea decked dark and beaded with moonlight. He considered everything, seeing details as they were, free of guilt and pain. Then he raised a hand and waved 'so long'.

AN IMMIGRANT'S
CHRISTMAS EVE

Stefania watches Michael as he sleeps. Three years old now, he looks more and more like her father with every passing day. Already, he has the same strong chin and the same way of wrinkling up his nose to laugh. There are times when she struggles to bring her mother's face to mind, but one glance at Michael and her father, Jozef, might just as well be standing there before her, large as life.

Tonight is Christmas Eve. Back in Tarnów this is the most precious night of the year, a night for family and all that family means, all the laughter, tears, tales and longings; but Ireland isn't Poland and tonight, sitting here in a bed-sit and watching her son as he sleeps, home has never seemed further away.

She sighs, a long tired breath that spins gossamer curls from her thin mouth. The cold has crept in only this week, turning everything ideally seasonal. For the past few days now, there has been a rawness to the air that makes smiling easier than usual. At the beginning she gave herself willingly to the spirit of things, braving the hectic streets, spending money she didn't really have on things that neither she nor Michael really needed. But that's Christmas.

Once the night-time has fully settled, she gives in and switches on one bar of the electric fire. An hour of that heat will make all the difference; if she is still feeling the cold after that then at least it will be late enough to go to bed. The apartment feels more bearable in the darkness. She draws her chair in close to the fire and sits forward all the way to the edge so that she is perched to savour the fullest throw of heat.

She has lived in this city for almost six years now, and Cork isn't so bad. Like a lot of her friends, she had listened to the stories of money to be made, of life to be lived and great adventure to be had. What she has isn't squalor, though it's a long way from the lavish world she'd been led to believe. But that's the way of the world. As it turned out, hers was the old story, that of tumbling headlong into love with a man who knew exactly the right way to flatter and coerce. For the better part of two years, his word was gospel and she feasted on the very sight of him, adoring everything from the premature salt-and-pepper sprinkle of his crew-cut all the way down to the caked mud of his steel-toed work boots. And when that bubble burst, her life had been changed forever. Well, she wasn't the first …

At home, they'd have the table laid for the Wigilia, the Christmas Eve dinner. Days would have been spent in decorating the house and preparing the many traditional meatless courses. Her father would lead the family in prayer, a place would be set in memory of their wayward daughter, and after the meal had been eaten, carols would be sung.

Tears form at a surge of childhood memories, and her throat tightens with a dehydrated ache. But instead of giving in, Stefania rubs her hands together, drawing in the yellow nourishment of the fire's heat, then stands and drifts around the bed-sit apartment, tending to small details by touch in the darkness. Christmas in Ireland is different than in Tarnów. If there is one lesson she has learned through all her mistakes, it is that regret is a useless emotion.

Michael is Irish. This, really, is the first year that he understands anything of the season. Tomorrow morning he will wake to a Christmas morning of presents carefully wrapped and placed underneath the small, decorated tree. His eyes will light up as she tells him that, because he had been such a good boy for his mummy this year, Santa Claus visited during the night and delivered very special gifts. They'll drink cocoa for breakfast as a special treat, then walk hand in hand to mass, smiling widely and wildly through the cold. And afterwards, he will play with his new toys while she cooks a dinner of roast chicken, sprouts and potatoes. This can be the start of a new tradition for them; their Christmas will be special because they have one another. Two is more than enough to make a family.

Stefania pulls her cardigan closed across her narrow chest, strikes a match and lights the candle that she has placed in the window. This is one of the traditions that Ireland and Poland share, and maybe the best one. A small, flickering glow, giving hope to wanderers everywhere.

THE CHRISTMAS LETTER

In our village, it was always Nonie Reardon who announced the coming of Christmas. As soon as the weather turned the right sort of cold, there she'd be, settling in for a fortnight's vigil, her wizened frame stooped in her doorway, her squinted gaze fixed up along the village as she waited for a certain good word. And that was the signal to everyone, not just the children, to begin the preparations in earnest.

Nonie was at the door and that meant Christmas was on its way.

When I knew her, she was a woman already well into her seventies, a lonely soul who lived mostly in her mind. Her home, the home of her mother's people, was a little two-roomed hovel of a cottage set beside the towering gates of the woollen mills. There had been a husband once, but briefly. They said he was a man from West Cork, Mick, and that he was tied up in that business with the crowd from the North. Nonie, the poor creature, had hardly been married when she found herself widowed; Mick had passed through in a hurry, though he'd paused long enough to leave her with his surname as well as the more lasting reminder of a kicking, screaming, bouncing baby boy. And what followed was the usual inevitable hardship, the struggle to survive, stretching the ends almost to snapping point in order to make them meet. It couldn't have been easy, but then, nothing was easy back in those days.

Anyway, all of that was before my time. When I first took notice of her, she was already old and had long since been left alone. All her relations were dead, and the boy, Michael, had taken off for England as soon as he was of an age. He had never returned.

Christmas moved something in old Nonie. The entire year seemed like a countdown to that one special day, and as soon as the first hard frosts stiffened the ground she'd emerge from her cocoon to take up her place in the doorway. We'd wave at her as we passed on our way to school, and sometimes, if she was not too distracted by her own rambling thoughts, she'd smile and wave back. Seeing her there, all frail corners and wispy hair, all bony hands tugging at the lapels of a threadbare cardigan, caused our world to shift, and we'd run off towards our classroom shouting as loud as our voices would go that, at long last, Christmas was coming.

She was waiting for a letter, of course. During the first few years after Michael's departure, he had been regular in writing home, and she would stop neighbours in the street to inform them of how he was getting along, what a success he was making of his life. As the letters arrived, the whole village followed his progress, and even felt some pride in his triumphs: the job he scored as a driver on the London buses; the small but notable promotion to inspector that followed within a few years; even his marriage to a girl from Mayo and the family that they set about building with all immediacy. Nonie lived for the arrival of those letters, and for the opportunity to share her son's latest news with anyone who cared to listen.

But while these brief updates were undoubtedly precious, they paled in comparison to the letters that arrived at Christmas. At the beginning the envelopes carried the splendid gift of money, rarely very much, just whatever he could spare, but to her it may as well have been a fortune in silver and gold. Then, after he was married, parcels began to arrive, maybe packing a new cardigan or headscarf, a box of chocolates, even a small ornament to be placed on the mantelpiece above the fire. Picking open the wrapping paper and folding it neatly away, Nonie became a child again. Her wide eyes glinted with the very essence of Christmas spirit set loose, and all the years of hardship fell from her in ropes.

After a few years, the flow of letters began to slow, running a month overdue at first, then longer. And finally a Christmas came and went without a parcel arriving. Morning after morning, Nonie filled her doorway and watched for the postman, but to no avail. At first mass on that Christmas morning, she knelt and prayed, and afterwards nodded and tried to smile as she passed out her season's greetings to everyone she met. Something had changed though. The glint in her eye was gone.

Throughout the years that followed there was never another mention of Michael. The proud boasts fell away and other things were discussed instead: the weather, the war, the price of potatoes. The neighbours, not wanting to embarrass her or open old wounds, took care that their words would not disturb the buried memory of her prodigal son. Such was life. And yet, when the next Christmas of loneliness rolled around, and all the Christmases after that, Nonie would again be seen filling her doorway, watching the road for the first sign of the postman, waiting, always waiting, for that letter. Every morning during that fortnight or so leading up to the big day, it was as if the clock had been turned back. She glowed again. Not with the brilliance of before, I suspect, but enough so that anyone who saw her had to feel at least a little of that magic for themselves.

As soon as I was old enough to notice this minor phenomenon, I asked my father about it. I could see neither sense nor reason as to why the old woman should build up her hopes in the face of almost certain disappointment. Perhaps keeping a vigil for the first few years was understandable enough, a lonely old soul so desperate for a friendly word that she was willing to close her eyes to her own obvious abandonment, but surely a time came when facts had to be acknowledged. Michael, her only son, was gone, and years had passed since the last attempt at contact.

My father gave a few moments of consideration to my question, then shrugged his big shoulders.

'Who knows, boy?' he said. 'While there's life, there's hope. Isn't that what they say? Maybe there's a grain of truth in that.'

I was disappointed with his answer, having been hoping for something a touch more substantial than such a throwaway platitude, but even at my youthful age I was beginning to understand that not everything could be easily explained.

My interest in Nonie refused to wane, even when other seasonal details started to vie for my attention, and I took to watching her at every opportunity. At the beginning, when she first took up her place in her doorway, the excitement stretched across that sunken face was clear to see. The harrowed eyes watched and waited, her bony arms crossing her chest, and I just had to believe her certainty was well-founded. This year, surely, the letter would come. But that day drew a blank, as did the next, and by the fourth or fifth day of waiting, the certainty began to waver. She shifted from foot to foot, licked her lips, crossed and re-crossed her arms, and it was actually possible to see her enthusiasm for Christmas slipping away. By the time we drew to within touching distance of the big day, I could see that she'd become a shell of her former self. Walking to school that morning, I decided that seeing her like this was quite possibly the saddest thing that I had ever witnessed.

An hour later, daydreaming my way through catechism lessons, a solution broke in my mind with such force that I almost tumbled from my tilted chair. As with all such answers this one seemed so simple: Why didn't I just write the letter myself and sign it from Michael?

There were flaws in the plan, and at ten years of age I was a long way shy of showing the least tendency towards genius, but I thought it would work. I knew she was anxious for a letter, and as long as I kept the details vague she probably wouldn't question too closely the disparity in handwriting.

So, that night, drawing on what little information I knew as well as what I could glean from a few casual questions put to my mother, I carefully tore a sheet of paper from my jotter and began to compose Michael Reardon's first letter home in many years.

It was no masterpiece. There was little I could say for fear of giving myself away, but somehow I managed to fill a page of joined-up writing with assurances that everything was just fine over here in England, that the wife and children sent their best wishes and that I was heartily sorry for letting so much time slip by without writing home. Trying to lend an authentic feel to the whole thing, I used 'Mam' whenever the opportunity presented itself, and I signed off with 'your loving son, Michael', hoping that I wasn't overdoing it. I folded the paper with great care, found an envelope in the chest of drawers in my mother's bedroom, and scrawled an address on the back.

I couldn't post the letter, of course. A letter sent from Ireland carried an Irish stamp, and that mistake would be instantly noticeable. But almost immediately I hit upon a solution. My mother had a brother who some years ago had emigrated to Birmingham, and under the pretence that I wanted to read his old letters, I pestered my mother into digging them out. Finally she did; anything for a quiet life, she said. She studied my face for the key to my lies, then sighed and warned me with the wave of a threatening hand to be careful with them. There were about twenty letters in all, some still in their torn envelopes. With the greatest of care, I picked off a withered stamp and glued it into place on Nonie's letter. It was smudged, and more than a little wrinkled, but I knew that it would do its job just fine.

The following morning was the day before Christmas Eve. A dusting of snow had fallen during the night, and all the children were out on the street, trying to scrape up enough of the stuff to make a snowman. I wanted more than anything to join them, but I forced myself to wait inside until the post had arrived. From our front window, I could see Nonie in her doorway, a rumpled, anxious shape with her hawkish face watching for the postman. I couldn't help smiling; this morning her long-awaited letter would finally arrive.

The eventual knock on the door brought nothing much, probably a few bills. I grabbed the letters with a muttering of thanks, fumbled through them and ran outside to watch who else might be receiving something in this morning's post. As usual, Nonie stood in her doorway before slipping inside when the postman approached to within a few houses. And as usual, the postman passed her on without so much as a glance.

I allowed ten minutes or so to pass, then made my move. At a determined pace, I marched up the road, conscious that the entire village was probably watching me and wondering what I was doing. Then I knocked on the door and stepped back to wait. From inside, I caught the small noise of movement, and eventually the door opened, Nonie's head and narrow shoulders emerging cautiously from the darkness. For a few seconds she stared at me, giving me the sense that she didn't know who I was, but then that blindfold cleared and she bent her mouth into a weary smile.

'Hello, boy,' she croaked, a question large across her face.

'Hi, Mrs Reardon,' I said. 'The postman just dropped off some letters to us, and I think we got one of yours by mistake.' I wanted to say more, but suddenly I was fully aware of my lies. Maybe, far from helping her by my deception, I was only torturing her. But I'd come too far to turn back. With a hand that had the cold as an excuse for its trembling, I held out the envelope.

Her eyes stared at the letter and her lips muttered something that didn't quite make it into actual words. Then, with a trembling hand of her own, she took it from me.

I cleared my throat. 'Well,' I said, wanting to add something. But there was nothing more to be said. 'Happy Christmas, Mrs Reardon,' I added as I turned away, but I'm not sure she even heard. She stood there for a few minutes more, utterly transfixed by the letter. Then she went back inside.

All that day, I was restless, wondering whether or not I had done the right thing. But the following day, Christmas Eve, I heard my mother telling Mrs Lenihan from next door that old Nonie Reardon finally got a letter from her son. Imagine, after all these years.

At mass on Christmas morning, everyone knew about the letter. Nonie could recite it by heart and did so at every opportunity. During the service, even Fr Murray took the time to give special thanks to the Lord for the mending of long-broken connections. In God's eyes there is no gulf too great to cross, he said, gazing down at where Nonie sat in one of the front pews, no separation that cannot be brought together again. I left the church with the feeling that I had been absolved of my sins.

Snow was falling again. The air was bitterly cold but everyone was smiling. Good wishes were passed around, and while the adults strolled back towards the village in little groups, chatting and swapping stories of years gone by, the children ran ahead, laughing and trying to catch snowflakes on their tongues. It was Christmas, and one that I'd always remember.

THE INNER LIGHT

From beneath the gauzy blanket of a dream, the old man felt something shift, compromising the stillness. He strained to listen, but the world was full of sounds that he'd only lately begun to hear, and it was a full minute before he caught the certain telltale sound of a floorboard's groan, the loose board on the landing just beyond his bedroom door.

'Jack.' His mouth shaped the name, a flicker of old tongue and a small widening of cracked and sunken lips, but the sound that wheezed to the surface was as dry and blanched as withered November leaves. Then, even before opening his eyes, he smiled.

Smiling really did make everything seem better. The air lost its stifling clamour and lightened around him, and even irreversible situations felt suddenly bearable. He held the smile until it had spread its rays out to the very furthest reaches of his face and delighted one more time in how the muscles tightened, how the creases of time flexed and deepened into the place of worthy shadow.

Then he opened his eyes on the half-lit day.

'How did you know it was me?' Jack stood in the doorway, small and impossibly young, a flower still a long way yet from fullest bloom. The glow of wonder at this piece of magic glimpsed lit a bonfire in his wide, heart-shaped face and made pools of his dark staring eyes, yet it was clear enough that he had reached a kind of precipice. Eight years old was childhood honed to a deadly edge, when all innocence felt distilled to its very purest form. At eight, every breath tasted of newly hatched summer, every bone ached to run. There was mystery to be found at every turn, the bristle and thrill of another challenge to be met and faced down. But all that chasing, laughing and playing had to lead somewhere.

The old man, the grandfather, shifted in the bed, then opened up that smile again. 'A trick I picked up over the years,' he said. He could feel the frail words flutter winged from his mouth, and almost expected to see them in flight. 'There are other things than maths and geography to learn, boy. And school won't have all the answers.'

Shyly, Jack approached the bedside, stood uncertainly for a second or two, then perched on the edge of the bed. The mattress barely sagged beneath his lithesome body. He stared at his grandfather, then took to studying what the fingers of his left hand were doing, how they bunched and built the white linen sheet into neat and even pleats. Two knuckles were skinned raw, the pale thin flesh pocked with a crust of scab. Fighting perhaps, or a careless careen against some pebble-dashed wall while in the fullest flight of some important game. Those were nasty wounds, yet of a kind quick to heal; a few wincing tears shed, a duty served, and then that stinging – surely the worst pain in the whole world – would begin to fade. Summer was calling, full as brimming wells with dew-laden mornings and joyous, rambling afternoons. There was time for tears, but not time to linger over them.

'Mammy's crying.'

The answering sigh had that same crumbling texture as the words. Naturally, being their raw ingredient. 'Is she? Well, mammies will do that sometimes.'

'She said that you won't last the night. I heard her telling Dad. She said you're dying.' Jack's voice seemed to snag on something then and jolt shut. He smoothed out the pleats that he had made, but the sheet wouldn't quite settle back to the way it had been before he touched it. When he spoke again, a dryness had crept into his throat, and the new words squeaked around their edges: 'Is she right, Granddad?'

The old man chanced a spurt of laughter and was pleased with the result. Over by the window he could see motes of dust fluttering in a veil of light, spores that danced and spun on vague draughts and spun again on stray, wandering breaths. 'She's as right as morning rain, boy.'

Jack looked up, caught between awe and terror. The old man could feel those child's eyes studying every fold of flesh, every jagged poke of bone, looking for an answer that felt like it just had to be there somewhere. Equal parts hoping and dreading a glimpse at the face of death itself. After a moment, he risked another question, his voice no bigger than before.

'Are you afraid?'

'Afraid?' The time was ripe for laughter again. 'Why would I be afraid?'

'But dying …'

With effort, the grandfather raised himself until he was sitting up in the bed. That felt better. Sitting up, he could see the window. A lot of things had changed over the past few years, the village where he'd grown up and grown old had shifted faces many times. But his bedroom window looked out across the fields and woodland to the west, and nothing much had changed out there. The patchwork hills still rolled in crests and troughs, the sky still scratched itself pale at dawn and set itself alight just before night came tumbling in. From this position, it was possible to believe that time had found a way of standing still, that the sun had crawled across the sky to bed down there night after night for simple fun and nothing more.

'Listen, Jack,' he said, just as he felt a wave of weariness rise and threaten to overcome his heart and mind. 'I'm sick. Way down inside, something's gone wrong. That happens, you know, and when it does there's nothing much than any-one can do. No point in crying about it or looking for some-one to blame. Just one of these things, boy. But it's made me awfully tired, and it hurts a lot if I don't lie still. Over the last few weeks the pain's gotten so bad, Jack, that it's living I'm afraid of now, not dying.'

Jack stared hard, then his chin began to jog with the effort at holding back a swell of tears, and when he bowed his head it was in surrender. The old man gave him time to cry, and he waited while minute tied to minute, each one seemingly precious now. When his voice came, it felt separated from his body, full of air, a long steady stream that whispered of its own accord, and he knew that it was as much for his own benefit as for his grandson's.

'At eight, you know, a boy takes pleasure in wasting time, because it feels enormous, incomprehensible, like it will never run out. And that is as it should be. Seconds to a child are like stars sprayed across the glass of a powerful telescope, and even though each one seems to bear a crumb of magic, a whisper of the unknown, each can be easily replaced by another once it burns out. But they stack up fast; those seconds somehow build into years, and by the time you realise that you'll have wasted towers of them.'

'I don't want you to die.'

Jack bunched the cuff of his shirt into one small fist and began to swab his eyes. His voice rode a stampede of hiccups, each a sword-thrust through his words.

'Well, if it helps, try not to think of it as dying.' He sighed, tired now, but happy too. 'Look.' It took great effort to raise a hand towards the window. The boy turned. 'See how when the light comes in at a certain angle all that dust starts to shimmer? It's beautiful really, isn't it? You step into a room and see that and your breath turns to stone in your chest, and you'll stand and stare at it for as long as you can, maybe until the light begins to wane again, and you won't quite understand why you feel the way you do. It looks nice, yes, but there has to be more to it than that, right? Now, look at it, enjoy it, but wonder what happens to those little specks of dust once the light falls away. Well, I'll tell you; nothing happens to them. They are there all the time. We just need a certain angle of light to make us aware of them.'

The boy stared, trying hard to understand, and the old man gave him time, though very soon now he'd need to dive back down into sleep. Already waves of exhaustion were lapping at his mind and he could feel the air around him begin to dim.

'There's more to us, you know, than bodies. If that was all we were, just skin and bone and a few pints of blood, we wouldn't be worth very much now, would we? No, our value is something untouchable, like time, and just like time it doesn't wear out. Our bodies are like flowers that grow with the sun and the rain, that bloom for a little while and then eventually wither and die. But the rest of us, the part that makes us who we really are, lives on. Just in another way. So, Jackie, after I'm gone, think about me like the dust in the room when the light has stopped shining. Just because you can't see me doesn't mean I won't be there. Okay?'

He closed his eyes, and for a while his sense of things began to drift away. The world around him held its breath and grew still, but one tether refused to break. Jack still sat there, watching, crying soundlessly, waiting for old to become ancient and ancient to become dust. The old man wanted to soar, but this one anchor was enough to keep him grounded.

'Won't you miss us?' the boy said, when his grandfather opened his eyes again. The young face was pointed with sorrow, grief scored eyes and mouth, revealing itself as a tension of posture. 'Won't you be sad about dying?'

'No, boy, I won't. How can I miss you when I'll see you all every day? This is my house. I was born here, I laughed and cried here, hid under beds, played games of hide and seek in these wardrobes. I've had great times and sad times here under this roof, I fell in love and grieved over loved-ones lost. I'm in every corner of this place, and I'm in you too, Jackie. Right now I'm sitting on an old man's bed looking out through a child's eyes at this shell that makes me sad to have to see. I beat a drum in your heart when you run and I tickle your mouth when you laugh. And downstairs I'm with your mother too, in her, listening while she talks and cries into the telephone, tasting the cup after cup of hot sweet tea that she likes so much. I might die an hour from now, or it might be during the night when all the world is fast asleep, but all that I am losing is my shell. Don't you understand that yet, Jackie? You and your mother have grown from me, and tomorrow and next year I'll still be running around inside of you both, just as a hundred years from now you and I will both be running around inside your children's children's children. Can you just imagine that, how wonderful life will be for us then? Time won't matter anymore, and we'll be eight or twelve or eighteen years old forever, a permanent prime. Dying is like being born, boy, a stop on a journey and nothing more. We have nothing to fear from that.'

He had closed his eyes again, and although a sort of joy shivered through his voice it was a soft, frail thing, as delicate and obscure as spun sugar. Jack watched as the muscles of that old, beloved face stretched out in one last smile, and then there was nothing more but sleep. Breaths came in thin hasps, barely enough to count for anything at all, and he counted, unhurried until he lost his way somewhere between seventy and a hundred, then he stood and crept from the room, careful not to make another sound. Behind him, the room seemed to shift, settling anew to its altered situation, but he ignored the urge to look back.

HEAVY SEAS

For a moment it had seemed as if they would hold their balance. The sky above was clear, dying towards black as the last edge of sun fell away and offering the first dim flash of stars off in the east, but a gale had blown for most of the evening and the ocean roiled, a swollen heave all deep troughs and great peaks that ruptured over and over in mud-coloured crescents. Pascal had been fighting to keep them upright, wrestling with the wheel, and Jacob could hear the low, desperate mutter of his prayers in between the wind's roaring gasps. Irish words, pleading to the Blessed Virgin, they filled the hollows of the falling night like music. The boat spun loosely on the churning sea, and there was that moment when it had seemed as if they'd make it, that their insignificance would somehow be their salvation, but then they took a broadside hit and it had felt like a wall coming down on them.

The rest was darkness, desperate flailing as the water closed in, its coldness crushing any effort at breath, coldness that destroyed its own taste and smell, everything.

Something odd had happened. Jacob thrashed and screamed, but he was engulfed by the grip of the sea. When he made the surface, the night opened up above him, and some incalculable distance away he caught a single flare of light as the last glimmer of sun careened off the final visible foot or so of hull and glistened on the water, and then the boat slid from view, the sun following it down. His breath beat hard in his throat and all around the wind rolled, drilling at the water, and he had never known a greater sense of desolation as he rose and fell with the turmoil of the sea, trapped in the thickening blackness. Gradually, his legs and arms were overcome by the cold and lost all feeling, and he floated because of the life-jacket, the orange padding swollen around him, holding him upright and alive.

Late the following afternoon one of the other boats found him. A miracle, everyone said, and it was; caught in a riptide, he could have been hauled far out from shore instead of drawn in an arc and taken back to within a mile of the island's most westerly edge. When the fishermen hauled him onboard he was conscious, though not for talking much. The boat was lost, he whispered, glaring past their faces and shoulders to check on a sky that still festered with the threat of further storm but which had mercifully found stillness, at least for now. The men understood and wrapped him in a piece of tarpaulin, all they had on board and useless really. One of them pressed a half-full flask of whiskey into his shaking hands and helped him to drink from it. He closed his eyes so that he might better savour the taste and also because it didn't do any good to see the deep dead spread of grey that had overtaken his fingertips nearly down to the first knuckle. His salt-encrusted lips bled around the flask's mouth and he gagged as the whiskey railed against his breath, but he didn't stop until every drop was gone, and then he lay back on the bed of the boat and slipped into a solitude of mind again.

There was something necessary about being alone. At home he kept himself mostly to the back bedroom. Around his family, he became ghostly. He ate the meals his mother prepared, or ate enough to assure everyone that he'd be all right, given just a little time. His mother couldn't help but worry, even after Dr Crowley explained that it was shock, that it would take some getting over a thing like that, such a tragedy. There had been concern over Jacob's fingers, and even greater concern about his feet, which steadfastly refused to bear his weight for days after he'd been taken from the water. The flesh was soft and discoloured, but a week of soaking in a warm water and mineral solution helped allay the worst of the doctor's fears.

By the middle of the second week it was decided to call off the search for the bodies of the other men. Jacob had given details of where they'd been fishing when the seas turned bad, of how they had been hunting for herring out along the rim of the sound about twelve miles south-southwest of the Calf Islands. But of course the swell had been treacherous, and they'd had a couple of hours at least of being hauled by the many cross-currents so it was impossible to guess with any degree of accuracy where exactly they were when the broadside wave had hit.

It was more or less accepted that the other men, Pascal Breathnach and Tommy Quinlan, had gone down with the boat. For the sake of the grieving families, it was better to believe that; under the sea, at least they were together and at rest. There was something less lonesome about that, somehow. Pascal, who shared ownership of the *Sorcha* with his sister-in-law, had been at the wheel during the worst of the weather, wrestling to keep them upright; Tommy had spent the last hours below deck, trying to keep the ballast from slipping. Jacob, as the youngest, had without discussion been given the short-straw duty of securing the nets and cargo crates, exposed to the worst of the elements. Short, with a low centre of gravity and possessed of broad shoulders and a strong back, he was used to the hardship of the sea, even at just twenty-two years old. Still, a couple of hours spent hunched against the sweeping gales and of fighting to keep his feet on the drenched and constantly pitching deck had worn him to the edge of exhaustion even before he had been thrown free by the collision wave. In the water, as the numbness took hold, it was almost a relief to give up and just wait for the end.

The men who came to the house held their black wool caps crushed in their big fists and looked around before settling for the fixation of the cold slab floor, and they thanked Jacob in whispers for his help, feeling ridiculous to be saying such a thing. No one suggested that he might join the search party, because it was better not to have to force a refusal from him. 'Well,' they said, nodding as they moved through the door, 'God bless', or 'take care, now', those who no longer kept religion, having seen the things they'd seen.

In the back room, he spread himself out across the bed and read old yellowed paperback westerns. He liked the simple clarity of the stories, the way good men were good and always did the right thing, and he liked the gaudy cover illustrations, with rearing horses, cowboys on the draw and scantily clad damsels in distress. The three or four hours at a time that he spent immersed in a Louis L'Amour was time spent wandering freely in another world. It was better, he discovered, to fill his mind with the words of other people.

'Your father's worried about you,' his mother said. He moved a potato across his plate and pressed the tines of his fork down amongst the slices of carrot, turning each piece from an orange penny into shapeless pulp. He glanced towards the corner. His father was sitting there with the newspaper folded up into quarters, studying the crossword, the stub of a pencil hovering and waiting to pounce.

'It's been a few weeks now,' she continued. 'He's afraid that you've gone into yourself. Isn't that right, Jack?'

In the corner, his father pursed his mouth, scrawled some answer into his crossword and then sighed with breathy satisfaction through his nose. He might have been alone in the room, but Jacob's mother chose to take the sigh as an affirmative.

'You're only twenty-two,' she said. 'You have your whole life ahead of you.'

Jacob nodded, tried to eat enough so that he could leave the room without a fuss. Later, he shaved himself in his bedroom, half-filling a dish with water heated on the stove and studying his face in the small six-inch square of wall mirror. The mirror was old; flecks of rust showed black around the edges where the glass had been worn thin by handling. His skin felt rough, his face an island face. Twenty-two, but already the sea winds had left their mark, creasing the flesh around his eyes and mouth and across his brow. In the weeks since the tragedy he'd lost a significant amount of weight; what remained hung heavily on his strong frame. He shaved and the face that looked back from the glass belonged to a stranger, only vaguely recognisable to his mind; he considered the features for a minute or two, tilting his chin one way and then the other for the fullest effect, then he dressed in his Sunday best and knotted a tie that he'd bought the year before on a trip to Cork city.

'I want to go into the village for a drink,' he said, standing close enough so that his father, sitting in the corner, was forced to acknowledge him. He could feel his mother standing in the doorway behind him and to the left, but he didn't turn. She'd be wearing her apron, maybe she'd be drying a mug or a plate with her 'Welcome To Killarney' tea towel. She was always either washing or cooking. The thought would be in her mind that she had pushed him too hard, that it was too soon yet to be getting at him, and he felt some undeniable satisfaction at the idea of her torment, though he could never have explained why.

His father looked up at him, pursed his mouth and nodded. 'Right, so.'

'Have you money at all?'

'What? Oh, money, yeah.' Jack dug in his pocket, drew out the handkerchief that he used to keep his money together. In amongst the oily folds, there was a ten-shilling note and some coins. 'How much will you be needing?'

Jacob didn't know. 'Enough to get drunk,' he said. Behind him, he could hear his mother's breath catch, and the muffled sound was her pressing the tea towel to her mouth in an effort to stifle a moan. Jack hesitated for just a second, then bunched the handkerchief closed and held up the bundle to be taken.

'Take care of yourself, lad,' he muttered, the words barely perceptible. Jacob nodded in a way that meant nothing.

Outside, a wind was blowing. The weather had shifted these past few days, and it leaned now from the northwest, bringing the first signs of winter. Jacob quickened his pace. It was a mile into the village, and it felt strange to be walking at this time of day. Not yet four o'clock, the boats would still be out. Ordinarily, he would have been too. He nodded to the few people he passed, but his pace deterred them from anything beyond a simple salute. They'd be thinking of the others, Pascal and Tommy, and even if they meant no harm at all, there was harm enough in such thoughts.

He walked on. Out in the harbour the ocean churned. The breeze flapped its irritation in the ash trees that huddled just behind the graveyard wall. There were a few boats tied up along the pier, but not many. Even with the weather, men had to work. Jacob sighed to himself, catching some of the sadness in the air. Maybe later he'd go for a swim. First things first though; he had a handkerchief full of money and thoughts that needed dimming.

A WORLD OF
DARK-HAIRED BEAUTIES

Once he stopped fighting the notion of boredom, Doug realised that it was in fact quite pleasant to be lying on this beach. The sand warmed him even through the tartan blanket he had spread, and when he closed his eyes against the glare of the afternoon the gush of the surf really was soothing to his mind. He lay there and felt the sun rash the bare flesh of his face, shins and forearms, and counted the minutes that it took for his body to relax from their usual tensions. An hour later he was startled awake by the scattershot of shrieks and wild giggling.

The sun had slipped behind a flash of mud-coloured cloud in a way that somehow bleached the sky. With effort, he propped himself up on his elbows, and glanced around. Christ, the sand looked soft, but wasn't. The muscles of his back cried out with every small movement. Twenty-three years old and here he was, knotted up like an old man.

Fifty feet away, a group of girls were trying to play volleyball without a net. There were other people around too, families and loners spread-eagled on the sand or wading waist-deep in the water, but none were as compelling to the eye as those girls. Six of them, all in their late teens or early twenties, tossing a mid-sized ball back and forth amongst themselves. Their noise continued, as determined as the rush of the waves, a nearly constant warble of laughter punctuated by loud, high-pitched whoops whenever one of their number went full stretch to make or miss a point.

Feeling new to the day, he lay there, propped up on his elbows, and enjoyed their movement and their partial nakedness, but in much the same way that he might have enjoyed studying a particular flower, or a painting in an art gallery. Their bikinis were old fashioned two-piece types that nicely showed off their shapes but which were not so brief as to be in any way really improper, and their incessant noise seemed to enhance their innocence. If they were on a cusp then they had yet to risk crossing over, and, for that reason, it felt okay to watch.

A breeze was blowing, slight but rather sweet. Earlier in the week it had been too hot to sit on the beach. He'd spent the first two days here trying to get drunk, but no matter how many cold beers he put away he couldn't seem to break through that final barrier. And his mother didn't approve of anything stronger. She didn't much approve of beer either, but he could see that she was making a special effort to keep quiet. Since he'd been discharged from the hospital she'd been smiling up a storm, to the point where the strain was beginning to take its toll. The beach had been her idea, hoping that it would do them both some good just to get away, to recharge the batteries and maybe come to terms with things. When he told her that his batteries

were dead, not just worn down, she had cried, the very
worst sort of tears, sad and silent. He'd watched, not saying
a word, but when he felt the first stirring of pleasure in his
chest he held up his hand and surrendered, pretending that
he was sorry and that it was a good idea, really it was. He
felt like a bastard for thinking some of the things that he'd
been thinking; none of what had happened was her fault.

When the sun burned through the cloud the girls threw
down their ball and went splashing out into the sea. They
moved in a pack, all fresh limbs and brilliant smiles. They
screamed at the chill of the water, took turns in plunging
under and leaping on one another. Doug watched them
and thought about a prostitute he had spent pocket-
money on in Saigon. She'd been nothing at all like these
girls, and he'd have bet his legs that she had never in her
life been able to laugh with as much freedom and lack of
inhibition. After twenty minutes or so they waded back
out of the tide, exhausted by their fun and games, and
staggered arm in arm up the beach almost directly in front
of him. He watched them openly, studying in the same
detached way as before how their skin glistened in the
sunshine. One of them noticed him watching and waved,
a brazen gesture that made the others bleat fresh new
gales of laughter again, but he nodded his head and tried
to smile.

'Enjoying the weather?' the brazen one asked, as the
pack skirted to within a few feet of where he lay.

He cleared his throat. 'A bit hot for me, but at least I'm
enjoying the view.' Even a year before, he'd have been too
shy even to look, but war had changed a lot of things.

'You a soldier?' one of the others asked. She was probably the pick of this bunch, with a slim face, polished tan and jet black shoulder-length hair that had been washed straight by the sea. She was feeding on the courage of her friend, but her large dark eyes gave away a delicious anxiety.

'Was,' he said, looking straight at her. 'Not any more.'

'Were you in the war?' Now another of the girls wanted in, but he kept his eyes fixed on the dark-haired beauty. She shifted under his gaze and, clearly uncomfortable, tried to slip back into the safety of her crowd.

'Yeah. I was up to my neck in it,' he said, hoping that they'd take that as a joke. They tried, but their laughter was limited to a few charitably nervous hiccups. They had come within a few feet now and could easily have passed on their way, maybe diffused the situation with another little wave or something, an easygoing so long, but one of them lingered, raising her left foot to brush sand from her toes, and perhaps it was the mention of the war that had awakened some sense of obligation. Or maybe they were merely curious.

He continued to study them openly; they had neat bodies, trim and shapely, but not movie star bodies or anything, nothing that would get them on TV. They were girls, seventeen or eighteen and predictably pretty because of that, pleasing to the eye. Sometimes, reality really did leave a lot to the imagination. They stood a couple of paces away, and he could see a slew of questions in their eyes, questions they were clearly afraid to ask. He considered them one by one, so slowly that it began to seem wrong somehow, before deciding that he'd been correct in his first choice all along, that the dark-haired girl really was the pick of the bunch.

'Well,' he said, when a cold smile began to crimp one corner of his mouth. 'So long, ladies. Don't let me keep you from your game.' Then he lay back on the blanket and closed his eyes. It was a moment before the sun fell across him once again, and another longer moment before he heard them a distance of forty or fifty feet off to his left, gathering up the ball and tossing it about once more. He waited for the sound of their laughter to settle into the afternoon, that tinny, clashing racket that would help to lighten the humid air, but their few efforts at mirth fell flat around him, like out-of-tune music. Not long after that, he was asleep once more.

He saw the dark-haired girl again at dinner. She was dressed in a pale blue cotton dress that did far more for her shape than the bikini had, and she wore her hair pulled back into a casual ponytail that really enhanced her face. A breeze from the nearby veranda caused the table's candle-light to flicker, and that soft, dancing glow seemed to out-line and emphasise the precision of her bone structure. When she saw him watching her she looked away quickly and began to fondle the lobe of one ear, but when she risked a second look, a minute or so later, he was still watching, and she offered a small, embarrassed smile before looking away again.

She was sitting with her family, her parents and a pinch-faced young boy of about ten or twelve who had to be her brother. The man to her left was bald and quite a distance overweight, and the woman across the table was small and dowdy-looking. They could have been a party of random strangers for all the likeness that they shared, but Doug understood that time was skilled in pulling at and reshaping surfaces.

The food was good, though a little too precise for his tastes. Poached flounder, asparagus, potato au gratin, some sort of rich white wine sauce. Perched at the bar with a hotdog and a cold beer would have done him just fine, but his mother had been at him since they'd arrived for an opportunity to dress up and today he was just too sick and tired of everything to bother even trying to put together another excuse. This was her vacation too, after all.

'Mabel said that just as soon as things pick up for Denny he'll get you sorted with some work,' she was saying now. The silver cutlery was tarnished from wear, but she held them in such an exact way that they might have been surgical equipment, scalpels and suture clamps, knife in her right hand, fork in her left, as if she were English or something. She'd painted her nails too, probably had used the chore to pass away the entire afternoon. The shade didn't suit her bony hands at all, the red so deep in this poor light that it might have been the maroon shade of freshly spilled blood.

'Should be set by the end of August. Mid-September at the latest, she said.'

If she noticed how his stare had locked itself away from her then she made nothing of it. He knew that she was afraid of some of the things in his mind.

Across the room, his dark-haired girl was fumbling at her ear again. A tiny pearl hung like a fast-thawing snowdrop from the underside of her lobe and glinted in the candlelight. Her profile might have been carved out of stone.

'What sort of work?'

His voice was vague, empty. The words filled gaps, nothing more.

'Oh, something in the shop, I expect. Does it matter?'

He watched his mother raise a sliver of asparagus and give it a second's consideration before eating.

'August, you say?'

'Well, August or September. Everyone's looking forward to having you home, you know, Doug.'

He nodded. The girl was trying to eat spaghetti. The breeze from the veranda must have stiffened with the fall of darkness, because now and again her hair fluttered, loose little strands of it corkscrewing up and outward before settling back down, less precisely, into place. But she hardly noticed, or maybe even enjoyed it.

'Yeah,' he said, softly, around a mouthful of fish. 'I'll bet they're counting the minutes.'

There was a moment then when he was certain that his mother was going to cry. She did that often, these days; the wrong word could send her down for an hour at a time. She never argued or screamed or shouted, or tried in any way to defend herself or to deflect the blows that the words delivered; she just bowed her head and gave way to silent, wretched sobs. He watched her face stiffen, thinking that she looked terribly old for forty-seven, as if her blanched flesh had set too tightly across her bones. She dressed these days in an eccentric, lost-generation style, and though she still dyed her hair, she never quite seemed to carry the effort all the way down to the roots. He watched her, waiting for the quiver of her mouth that would signal the breakaway of tears, but it was possible that she had already cried herself out for the day.

'Mabel's your sister,' was all she said, her voice a dry wisp, not quite a cough, but nearly. 'You know how much she loves you, Doug.'

He thought about asking just how much Denny loved him, Denny, his sister's husband, who flew a flag on his porch and boasted an Uncle Sam decal in the back windshield of his Camaro, but who escaped the draft by sticking a sharpened pencil an inch and a half into his left ear. Denny, a guy who had drunk away every weekend since he was probably sixteen years old and who liked to keep his wife in place with a twice-a-month shot to the kidneys, and maybe a kick or two if someone had made fun of him or dared to question one of his tall tales down at Kelsey's bar. But there was nothing to be gained with a question like that.

'Yeah, well, I'm not so sure that shop work will suit me all that much,' he said, as much to himself as to his mother. 'I've been thinking about taking a trip.'

'You mean like a vacation?' His mother pushed her plate away, just a few inches, but the intention at abandonment was clear.

'Like one,' he answered, letting his stare range out over the room again, out to where his dark-haired girl sat wrestling with her spaghetti. 'But not one.'

'I don't understand.'

He shrugged. 'I don't much either, to tell you the truth,

Ma. But I do know that I don't want to spend the rest of my days sitting in a shop while Denny spins his ropes of bullshit.'

There was more to be said, on both sides, but he couldn't find an order for the words just now and, clearly, neither could his mother. He watched the girl across the room and listened to the incessant pulling and unfurling of his mother's whispered breath beside him. When a waiter drifted within hailing distance he made a gesture and ordered Scotch on the rocks, twice. His mother set down her cutlery with more noise than they should have made, but she offered nothing in the way of objection.

They worked at the whiskey in long steady sips, and the only noise worth noting was the cracking of the ice cubes in the alcohol and an occasional clicking as they bounced against the walls of the glass. When he was most of the way through his drink, Doug raised a hand and signalled the waiter to bring them two more.

'Do you know that girl?'

He turned, trying not to be abrupt, but the set of his face defied him and he didn't quite trust himself to speak. His mother met his eyes without flinching, only her slatted lips working with the taste of the Scotch.

'You've been watching her all night.'

'She was at the beach today. With her friends. We exchanged a few words, that's all.' He turned back to study her again. The family had finished with their main courses and were studying the dessert menu now. Apart from the girl, they looked like people who didn't spend a lot of time worrying about diet.

'Don't do this to yourself, Doug.'

'Do what?'

'You know what.'

He smiled, a little twisting of the mouth that jarred the lips apart to reveal tightly clenched teeth. 'I know,' he said, 'but I want to hear you say it.'

'There is a big wide world full of dark-haired beauties, but stop torturing yourself. And, for Christ's sake, stop torturing me, okay?'

She finished her Scotch in a rush. 'Don't you think I blame myself enough for what happened? Don't you think my world came apart the same as yours did when I heard the news, Doug? You're my only son. A better mother would have stopped you from going, would have found a way of getting you to Canada or Mexico. Knowing that has eaten a hole inside me. But what's done is done. The world won't change for wishing. You've earned the right to be bitter, God knows, but hating every single turn of the world won't help you to live in it. At least you're alive. You might not think that's much of a consolation, but it is. Believe me, it is.'

A waiter floated into view again, ready to freshen the drinks once more. She leaned back and let him take the glasses. Her hands shook visibly on the table, and to busy them she began to worry the white lace fringe of her napkin.

'Just give it some time. Nothing can turn back the clock, but if you'll just sit back you'll realise that there are other things in life besides that.' She took her third Scotch from the waiter without the slightest acknowledgement of the young man's presence, and sipped from the glass, sluicing the whiskey not quite silently through her teeth and holding it a long moment on her tongue before swallowing.

'Of course, I can't very well stop you if you're absolutely determined to go off travelling, but running isn't the answer. Just give it a year or so. You don't have to go to work with Denny. I'm sorry, I didn't mean to push you. I just thought, well, I'm not sure what I was thinking. That a job might help you get your mind off things, I guess. But forget about that. You'll have your pension. Maybe you might feel like trying a college course or something.'

He slept for an hour, maybe two, a tossed, broken sort of sleep that was about as good as it got for him anymore. Spokes of pale light made it through the window from the poolside down below, and he lay back in the strange hotel bed and wondered how many lovers had held one another under these sheets. Images flickered through his mind, but they were nothing new, the edges of their terror tempered by familiarity. He knew what was real and what was not, because what was real was worse.

It was wrong to pray for death; he knew that without having to be told. In the hospital, they had tried to have a chaplain speak with him, hoping that something good might come of it, but what could any priest or rabbi have said that would make things better? The chaplain had been a young man of probably mid- to late-twenties, tall and stoop-shouldered, unaccountably nervous in his mannerisms. He had spoken in a slightly rote way about God's reasons being a mystery, but his voice was reedy and full of grace notes, and a lot of what he said felt like lip service. 'Faith is easier to keep when the hand being dealt is a pat one,' he had said, just before he left, which was about the only thing really worth saving from his twenty-minute visit.

Everything felt different now. The war had taken in a young kid and sent home a feeble old man, or not even that, but the shell of a man. A husk. At twenty-three, he should have only been beginning to live, but what stretched out before him now felt like waiting time. No matter how hard he tried, he couldn't imagine how things would be for him two years from now, much less twenty. But he no longer cried about it. There was that, at least.

The image of the dark-haired girl flushed through his mind. Not as she had been on the beach, all gentle curves and revealed flesh, but the way she had looked in the dining room at dinner. Her hair pulled back, careless and carefree, to sharpen the beauty of her face; her large dark eyes still innocent but just beginning to learn; and her perfect body ripe and ready in that sleeveless pale blue cotton dress. He imagined how it would be to kiss her, deciding that a kiss from her couldn't be all that different from the kisses of other girls that he had known. Yet, for some reason, he knew that it would be different. As the fantasy-her drew back slowly from him, her smile locked itself in and awakened a distant ache that could do nobody any good, but the darkness made him vulnerable to such feelings and there was nothing he could do but lie there and wait for its passing.

His mother was right: running was not the answer. The truth was that there were no answers. His clammy skin caught a hint of draught from the open window. It wasn't much, but he tried to make the best of it. This hurt was his to bear, and the pain would either subside in time, or it wouldn't. The trick, a soldier had told him, back in the hospital, was to clear your mind of bad thoughts. 'Try thinking about lawnmower engines, or football, or give praying a try.' An old soldier with a long, drawn face, pasty skin and the sad eyes of a beaten dog. 'In time, your mind will stop obsessing about it, and you'll feel better in yourself.' The operation was all about containment now.

Doug held to the stillness of the night for as long as he could bear, then struggled free of the bed sheets, sat himself up and snapped on the reading lamp that craned up and out from the locker to his right. He peeled off his T-shirt and tossed it across the room. It caught the back of the desk chair and held for just a moment before losing its grip and tumbling to the floor. He stared at the puddle it made there and out of habit ran one hand across his stomach, the tips of his thumb and index finger tracing the nest of scars. Then, without thinking much, he closed his eyes and slid open the locker's drawer.

At home, he kept a gun there, had done so ever since his father's passing. Jesus, that was almost ten years ago now. His mother had never liked the idea of a weapon in the house but, as the man of the family, he felt that he had to do what was best for them all. So, he had moved it from his father's bedside locker to his own. In truth, he wasn't all that sure that the thing would even fire if ever called upon, but simply knowing that some sort of protection was within easy reach did help to sate the worst of his fears during those first long wintry nights when every settling floorboard and contracting water pipe seemed like the determined creep of an intruder.

Since then, it had remained tucked away in that drawer, in amongst the general clutter of letters, a long-abandoned stamp collection, a few creased old baseball cards and various other little souvenir nothings of his teenaged years. An old Beretta Jetfire. Occasionally, a long way into some sleepless night, he liked to reach out in the darkness and slip his hand inside the drawer, to fumble his knowing way past the crumpled cards and papers and just settle his grip over the gun to find comfort in that familiar shape and weight, in the cold, oily touch of all that killing iron. This was a hotel room, though, just a place by the sea a long way from home, and when his hand made it inside the drawer now there were no papers or postcards to meet his touch, no chunk of handgun either. He rubbed his fingertips slowly along the bottom of the drawer, feeling the grain just an edge above true smoothness, until in towards the back his touch bumped the waxed-leather spine of a Gideon Bible. With hours of time to kill until dawn, he lifted it out and let his hands enjoy the cracked touch of the moulded blue covers. Then he lay back down in the bed and opened the book to a random page. He didn't know anything about lawnmower engines, and baseball had always been his game, not football.

AFTER THE HEIST

Everyone had gotten away clean. We followed the plan, went our separate ways and got busy laying low for a while. But something somewhere had gone wrong and, on the third day, Johnny Cassano turned up dead.

Since Monday, the headlines had been full to splitting with details of the heist. CNN had just about fallen over themselves to deem our job 'the most audacious raid in American banking history,' and the *New York Times* devoted seven full pages of their Tuesday edition to analysing this 'modern-day Jesse James adventure'.

Virtually round the clock for two days and nights, every so-called expert in the fields of security and economics was dug up and made to sit in plush studios to debate the crime, and though their voices were sober and measuring, holding with discipline to the facts as they saw them to be, they seemed, to a man, to glow with awe at the sheer magnitude of what had happened. They were impressed, everyone was; it simply beggared belief that a gang of five men could walk into Manhattan's largest bank, dressed in blue overalls and wearing clown-face make-up but armed with nothing more evident than a slip of paper, and in less than ten minutes, carrying sacks crammed nearly to spilling with tens of millions of dollars, stroll back out and just disappear into the height of rush-hour traffic. No alarms had been raised, no one had lifted a hand to try stopping their escape. Surely, such a stunt had to be impossible, and yet that is exactly what had happened.

The note was brief and straight to the point: 'This building is wired. Empty the vaults or we detonate.'

Nobody bothered to argue with that.

I followed the news reports because I needed to do something to help kill the time, and also because this spinning out of the whole saga did make for enjoyable viewing, but I refused to let myself buy too deeply into all the Hollywood-styled hyperbole, and I did my best to keep my head from swelling too much.

Predictably, the figures bandied about on screen and in the papers were wildly divergent from one another, with the most conservative estimates (*USA Today*'s) putting the stolen tally at $112 million, a full third higher than the true amount. It was as clear as a ringing bell, to me anyway, that we who had gotten our hands dirty were not the only thieves in this game. Everyone steals from everyone else, right on down from the very top.

Then came the business with Johnny Cassano, and that changed everything. What had until then been audacious and impressive, suddenly became a sordid, bloody mess.

I caught the story on the late news. At first, he was just a piece of incidental gossip, a man found garrotted in a

Wal-Mart parking lot down in Freehold. They had a name, Cassano, and reports placed him as a loose affiliate of the Gambino Family. But within an hour, somebody in the research department had unearthed a more solid crime-syndicate link, and from there it was only a matter of time before Cassano would be connected to the week's major news headline: the New York bank heist.

He had refused to stick to the order. When he was supposed to be lying low, the stupid son of a bitch was spotted down in Arlington, at the track, throwing around five-grand bombs on the longest shots he could find. And good losers were a flashing neon sign; they raised eyebrows in a hurry. We all knew that the Feds would be watching, and that they wouldn't be limiting their attention to any list of most likely suspects, either. On a job of this magnitude, they'd have eyes for everyone who had ever stretched out to vacation in the pen, anyone who had ever even nodded hello to the wrong sort of people. There was one simple rule to follow: don't attract attention. Don't be seen overspending on as much as a loaf of bread; don't go working the champagne-shift at one of the uptown nightclubs; don't even jaywalk, for Christ's sake. A month of lying low wasn't too much of a hardship, not when you considered the reward. A month or maybe six weeks, tops, and then we were all home free. We all knew the score, and it should have been the simplest thing in the world to just lie low and daydream of pots of gold at the ends of rainbows. But Johnny had screwed even that up.

Someone had caught up with him, at great risk to themselves, and dragged a piece of cheese wire through his windpipe, right there in a Wal-Mart parking lot. I knew that, even as the news spun its latest twist in the tale, the police were probably pouring over reams of surveillance tape, interrogating anyone who might have fallen within a fifty-mile radius of Freehold in the day in question, and slowly, methodically, drawing up a list of known associates. They didn't give a dime-store damn about him personally, of course; in their eyes, a man like Johnny Cassano was scum and deserved every stinking slice of bad luck that fell his way. No, their interest in him was purely mercenary. Someone had wanted, maybe needed, to shut him up, permanently, and they just had to know why. So, he had become the chump bait that could possibly snare a multimillion-dollar catch. For the first time in his entire rotten life, he had become a valued member of society.

By the Thursday morning, CNN had been pushed into a leap of faith. They announced a second gangland slaying; this time, Giovanni Mezzo, better known in underworld circles as 'The Driver'. Apparently, gunshots had been reported at a building in the Bronx, and police had arrived on the scene to find Mezzo dead in the service elevator, shot seventeen times at point-blank range. Listening to the report, I knew that the newsreader, a hot blonde with a smoky tone, was flying high by the seat of her delectable and perfectly-filled pants; that the ropes she spun to connect 'The Driver' with Johnny Cassano were as thin as cobweb and just about as full of spider's shit.

According to Miss Pretty Fine, Cassano and Mezzo had both once been pulled in for questioning over a Vegas execution. Fourteen years ago, that was, and neither had been officially charged. It was a shakedown, nothing more, one of those routine but relatively minor irritations that filled a regular gap in the course of a wiseguy's daily toil, but even tenuous links could be implied to mean something. The blonde beauty on the screen was selling snake oil, her words saying one thing, her demeanour and her knowing silences adding the critical details, the ones that nailed coffin lids shut.

I knew that there was nothing to the reporter's claim. The truth was that our job had been crafted down to the most minute detail over two solid years. Every angle had been covered and great care was taken to ensure that none of the five men were in any way acquainted, not by blood, not by circumstance, not even by reputation. Each man had been recruited for a particular skill as well as for calmness during a big game, and each was solidly reliable in a pinch; they were drawn from cities all across the country, nominated for consideration by their respective Families. There was no room for loopholes, and no nooses that might be used to hang anyone connected with the job. CNN, maybe under duress from the Feds, were making news out of a few scattered jigsaw puzzle pieces. They were blowing hot air, and yet, somehow, and probably without even realising, they had happened on something decidedly close to the truth.

Yet suddenly, just four days after the event, our number had been reduced to three. I knew that the others would have been following the news reports with a diligence close to my own, and I believed I knew what they'd be thinking. Someone was taking out the gang, one at a time, either because the idea of sharing the loot no longer seemed so appealing, or because whoever had organised all of this was worried that the hands-on witnesses might be persuaded to talk, given enough of a squeeze. Two men were already dead, and any one of us could be next.

But what was there to do? A phone call now might trigger exactly the wrong response, especially when anxiety would have already entered the picture. And besides, there was no telling who might be listening. I watched the latest updates spin themselves new strands, each adding a little more colour than the last, and decided that it might be best if I gave things twenty-four hours. That would be enough time for the situation to settle down, and for common sense to prevail. I made spaghetti and meatballs, put on some music and resolved to sit tight.

At four a.m. the phone rang. I hadn't been asleep, but I didn't hurry to answer. A call at that hour wouldn't be full of joyous news, and the longer I delayed in picking up, the more time I'd have to fill with blissful ignorance. But it couldn't be ignored forever, and this caller was insistent and stubborn. Ten chimes, then fifteen, a pulsing metallic quiver that made splinters of the night. When I could bear it no longer, I lifted the receiver.

'Yeah.' I stood in the darkness, gazing out through the window at a lost world. The ocean was out there somewhere, and a breeze, which had kicked up some time in the last few hours, sent scuds of cold rain lashing against the glass.

'Cobb's dead.'

I inclined my head and closed my eyes, just for a moment. When I opened them again, the room seemed to have bled a little brightness from somewhere. Everything was shades of grey.

'What the hell are you doing? This phone could be covered.'

Farina sounded far away. A second's delay seemed to fall between every phrase. Dumb guinea, I thought, suddenly weary to my very bones. He suffers a bout of panic and I get compromised. In ten minutes flat, I'd need to blow this place, try to hustle my way to another safe house. That time delay was a bad sign.

'Did you hear what I said. Cobb's ...'

'I heard. Now, what's your problem?'

That delay again. Then: 'Jesus, Paulie. He's the third one. Now there are only us two left. And you took so long answering the phone, I thought, well ... Jesus.'

Anger swelled up inside of me, a consequence no doubt of having been cooped up for days in this crummy bed-sit apartment. 'What the hell's the matter with you, huh? You got wood for brains? Bad as this place is, it keeps the rain off my head. Now, thanks to you and your case of the jitters, I have to bail out. If you want some free advice, you might want to think about doing the same.' I sighed, hard. 'I don't get it. Everyone said you were a stand-up guy, that you wouldn't come apart no matter what kind of shit came down on you. And yet, here you are, bawling like a kid with a skinned knee.'

That was the kind of talk that, under normal circumstances, would have put him in a hard spin. Right about then, it wouldn't have surprised me to catch the hiss of his fuse burning down. But he was scared and it was as if my words didn't so much as touch him.

'Three of us down. Don't you see what that means, Paulie? Two to go. There's just you and me, and the bullet could be coming from any direction.'

There was no use in arguing. He had set his mind to it, and I knew his type well enough, had been around men like him my entire life, just about. So I listened. What else could I do? Words built on words, one thing leading to another.

He was hesitant in saying the last part of what was really on his mind and I had heard enough to know that pushing him would be a colossal waste of good escape time. I put up with a good five minutes of panic-talk, all the while packing my case one-handed and keeping a close watch on the coast road outside. A gun lay on my pillow, an untraceable stub-nosed Colt, loaded and cocked, already dressed for the party. Loud and messy, it was a beautiful weapon. The first sign of a visitor and I could be away in a hurry, and if necessary spraying all manner of hell before me.

'Listen Paulie, I've been doing some thinking, you know. You and me, we're in the same fix, don't you think? Whoever took out the others will be wanting to pay us a visit too.' Farina paused, and then plunged headlong over that cliff. 'What would you say to the two of us teaming up?'

'The plan was to lie low and not to make contact with one another. Under any circumstances.'

'Screw the plan,' he roared. 'I'd say the situation has changed a little. Wouldn't you?'

I thought about that. 'Go on.'

'The way we are now, whoever wants us dead can come and pick us off whenever he wants. But together, we'd be a different proposition. We can still lie low, but together we'll be able to watch each other's back. What do you say, Paulie?'

He was running scared, all right, but that didn't mean to say he wasn't making a good point. And he was right about one thing: the rules had changed.

'I'll need to make a call,' I said at last.

'I don't think that's such a hot idea. Look, I don't know who's behind this, but whoever it is, they want us all out of the picture. Now, I'm not pointing any fingers, and it could just as easily be my crew plotting this as yours, but I think that, for now anyway, we should give serious consideration to playing this one close to our chests. A week under every radar, maybe we'll dig up a few facts. Maybe we'll even smoke out whoever it is that wants us dead.'

I took a few seconds to think. Out on the coast road, I caught the distant glimmer of headlights rounding a corner. Just a flash, and then they were either doused or were smothered by another twist in the road. I snapped my suitcase shut and picked up the gun.

'All right. Meet me in two hours.'

'Where?'

'That place, out by Trudy's.'

'The yard?'

'Yeah.'

'Two hours.'

I showed up early, checked out the site for possible ambushes. We'd used the place before, a vacant lot cluttered up with a couple of rusted-out cars, some heaps of rubble, a spew of broken glass and a lot of weeds. I parked and slouched low behind the wheel, keeping the silence. Dawn broke unseen; the bank of rain cloud was too well settled and the cold kept everything on a knife-edge.

Just before seven, a coffee-coloured sedan floated by. It circled the block, slowly, and I appreciated the effort. Maybe I'd misjudged Farina, maybe he had just been spooked. Well, he had a right to be. And at least now he seemed to be thinking clearly again. Caution was an admirable character trait. A couple of minutes passed, then the sedan reappeared, and this time eased in off the road. He drew up close, parked snugly on my left, and killed the engine. I hesitated, gave myself the small assurance of the Colt barrel's chill touch in my jacket pocket, then stepped out and hurried around to his car's passenger side.

'Some setup, huh?' he said. The strain was clear in his voice as well as in the pallid jowls of his face. He tried to smile, showing a lower row of small neat teeth, but the expression did him no favours.

I shrugged in reply, reached out and lowered the volume on Frankie Valli.

'You blow your safe-house?'

He nodded. From the way he looked at me, it was clear that he was content to let me call the shots. Well, that was fine by me. I hunched against the cold and, watching the rain smatter against the windshield, told him that I knew of a place, a fair distance out of town, but safe. I'd vouch my life on it.

'You are,' he said, but that was a wisecrack without any real intent, nothing more than a reflex action. I explained that the safe house was the summer place of a lawyer that

I had in my pocket. It was ideal for what we needed: small town, set back from the main road, two clear ways in and out, cosy but plenty big enough for two. 'No one will get the drop on us, up there,' I said, and Farina studied me and decided, at last, to believe it, a decision made easier by the knowledge that he didn't have much in the way of choice. It was either dance to my tune or dance alone, and he was too far gone for that.

'We may as well get moving,' I said. 'We're looking at the bones of a four-hour drive. If we get separated on the highway, there's a truck-stop joint outside of Henderson. We can meet there.' Then I wrestled the door open and stepped out, grimacing hard against the rain. The past few minutes had done their part in breaking up the worst of the darkness, but out on the road a street lamp still burned in a way that set the sodden ground to shining. I bunched my jacket tight around my throat and moved at a jog around the back of the sedan to my own car. Just as I reached my door, I heard his engine rumble to life and gun once, and I turned, as if remembering something. Farina looked up, and began to wind down the window in anticipation of my words. I drew the gun from my pocket and shot him in the face, twice, keeping just enough distance to avoid taking on any of that mess.

An hour later, I was out of state. The rain stopped, but the sky refused to clear. The horizon line lay swollen and bruised, with the promise of worse up ahead. Well, that was all right. I could handle a little rough weather. I drove, keeping to a steady sixty, with the radio tuned to an oldies station, and listened without spending much on concentration to a parade of Roy Orbison, the Beatles, the Stones and Creedence Clearwater Revival, songs that fit a comfortable place in my mind.

Everything had gone exactly according to plan, every single step of the way. Farina had been the easiest of the four to kill, dispatched with those two close-up shots, the second unnecessary as anything other than a slice of insurance. His eyes had seemed to bulge with a glare of shock in that instant before I pulled the trigger, and even though I questioned whether I had seen that or merely imagined it, because there had hardly been time, not even a split second, for him to piece together the entire score, I understood that it would etch a permanent mark in my memory, one to be revisited in the small hours of distant nights. Still, an occasional ghostly visitation was a small price to pay for the jackpot I had hit.

Eventually, they'll come looking. I am, after all, dealing with people who don't easily forget a slight. I realise that the whole thing was quite a stunt – the heist, obviously, but the string of executions too. Maybe the executions even more so than the heist. There will be a lot of anger in certain circles as soon as all the details emerge, but I plan to be long gone by then. My reasons for hiding are pretty much the same as my reasons for stealing and then killing. If I am ever asked, I can reply, truthfully, that those reasons number somewhere in the region of about seventy million, and I really do feel that such a figure provides more than ample motivation for keeping my head down and staying forever out of sight.

IN TOO DEEP

After a while, Fr James opened his eyes and just lay motionless in his bed, no longer fighting the insomnia. His throat felt parched with the sort of thirst that could be terribly dangerous for a man like him, but even though there was a tap not twenty feet from where he lay, he refused to get up, refused to disturb the rut that he had forged in the corn-shuck mattress. He held his place, hardly even breathing, and listened to the slapping of the ocean against the broken shore until, at last, some strain of music began to emerge, the gentle sway of a bel canto beneath the slow cadenzas of a breeze.

Then, suddenly, he could bear the stillness of his room no longer and he leapt from the bed, hurried through to the pantry and splashed some whiskey into a cup. Not much, just a tot, but he swallowed it hard and then stood there, hip braced against the counter-top, panting. The whiskey ripped through him, bringing that familiar heat. He filled the cup with tap water, emptied it into the sink and then rinsed and emptied it again. Mrs Kelleher, who looked after the rectory, was thorough when it came to cleaning, conscientious far beyond the call of duty, and he knew from experience that the less fuel that he gave her for village gossip, the better.

The whiskey unnerved him. To escape the clutches of the bottle, he took to drifting around the dark house, moving from room to room, sometimes lingering to gaze out at the night that lay beyond. Whenever he listened, really listened, he could hear the ocean. And he was at the great old casement window of his living room, peering out past his own vague reflection into the darkness and turning melodies out of the music of the night, when the clock on the mantle struck three.

Without thinking very much about what he was doing, he went outside and stood barefoot in the garden. Rain had fallen some time in the past few hours and the long grass was cold and sodden, the earth beneath clammy. The breeze was strong, rustling the roadside alders and moaning in the eaves of the house, and rags of cloud dragged across the sky, obscuring stars for seconds at a time, blurring the pale conch moon that slouched low in the south.

Fr James was tall, almost six foot, though with a notable drooping of the shoulders that gave him a beaten, almost cowardly, stance. Thin far past the point of gaunt, he looked quite a bit older than his age of forty-two should suggest. His face wore an expression of permanent strain, his slatted mouth working ceaselessly at trying to shape some impossible or unutterable words, and his grey eyes stared with an intensity that hinted at some medical trouble; an overactive thyroid, perhaps. He always seemed somehow ill at ease with daylight, and was one of those men better suited to the hours of darkness.

No one had accused Fr Larkin of anything yet – not outright, at least – though there had been whispers, and he saw the way that people looked at him. Already, the police had questioned him, but that was hardly much of a surprise. Fr Larkin was well into his sixties and boasted what could most charitably be termed a colourful past. Most pertinently, there had been that business with the woman. The smallest amount of mud, they say, leaves a stain.

Still, questioning was one thing, proof quite another. And, so far, the boom had yet to fall.

The cold didn't touch him, though it was mid-November. He could still taste the sharpness of the whiskey at the back of his throat and, also, the memory of its heat. A few spatters of rain began to fall, though they were sparse enough to raise some doubt about the matter, but instead of returning inside, he walked around to where his bicycle leaned against the side of the house, and climbed on. A quick wander through the village often helped to alleviate the worst of his tensions; the stormy rush of air pummelling his face, filling his lungs, had a magical way of revitalising his tired mind. No one would think it strange to see him hurtling through the streets at this time of night; these small hours where invariably when sick people chose to die, and a priest's duties were never limited by the confines of a usual working day. So, he was free to cycle where and when he wished, but tonight, for some reason, that freedom didn't feel quite enough.

He reached the edge of the village in a matter of minutes, considered turning back for home, then on a whim decided to keep going. The road wound out along the coast, a single narrow lane all overgrown by ditches of haw and shedding sycamore, and with every twist the darkness seemed to swell to an even greater depth. He didn't think about where the road would lead, didn't want to care, just then, about such things. He simply cycled, enjoying how the slack muscles of his legs strained to push the pedals, and remembering how, as a boy of perhaps ten or twelve, he and his friends would often sneak away in the night-time to go swimming. Children have one set of fears, adults entirely another. Neither he nor his pals had worried about the dangers of drowning, just as they never thought to fear such real-world threats as heart attacks or strokes. Instead, they exchanged ghost stories, reciting as sworn testimony their fathers' or their grandfathers' encounters with the Banshee, or the Pooka or the Coach de Bower, the Death Coach, and wrapped in the delicious dread of those tales, they shivered and threw darting glances at the road that stretched behind them or searched the pitted blackness between the leaning trunks of trees for the vaguest hint of some terrible watching face. Fear had held such an element of fun, back then.

He recalled that the swimming on those nights as being especially invigorating, how the very blood in his body had prickled with such joyous cold, and every worldly worry seemed to just fall away as unimportant, because all that truly mattered was staying afloat, trying to breathe, trying to wrestle against the currents and the tidal sway. The rules of the game had been simple: survive.

A couple of miles outside the village, the road bent away

from the coast and twisted inland, leaving only a small rutted pathway, a boreen, to continue down towards the shoreline. Without the least hesitation he steered his bicycle onto the rough surface, slowing his speed just enough so that he might guard against punctures or unexpected changes in the terrain. He held the vague idea of enjoying a stroll along the shoreline. Or perhaps he'd even roll up the legs of his trousers and allow himself the pleasure of a paddle; after all, his feet were already bare, and the salt water might do them good. But when he reached the beach and surveyed the situation, he saw that the sand stretched hardly more than fifty yards or so before it hit a rocky wall of shale, and the option of a walk no longer seemed to offer quite the level of fulfilment that he had imagined.

The sky had completely clouded over now, and there was no light to be had at all. Even the moon was lost. The breeze, too, had stiffened into a strong westerly wind; it sluiced through the rocks and buttresses, its gusts moaning canticles of disquiet. And all the time, the ocean beat against the shore, darkly brooding and bullying with its heavy swell, breaking in feathers that hung for long moments in gossamer reels across the dim sand. He stood there at the top of the beach, absorbing the details of the night, then hurriedly peeled off his clothes. In his priestly garb, his flesh had all the sallow hue of newly churned butter, but naked he turned a milky shade of pale and seemed the night's brightest offering.

Feeling like a boy again, he ran down towards the water, waded quickly out to a depth chest-high and plunged under. A moment later, he resurfaced, flailing to stay afloat and fighting for breath against the engulfing cold. When he regained his composure, he stretched out in a clumsy but effective freestyle stroke, and began to crawl out to a greater depth. The water was rough, and he could feel currents dragging him this way and that, wanting to haul him under. He tried to rise with the waves as they came, because to struggle against them could wear you down in a hurry, but even out here, some thirty or forty yards from the shoreline where the fullness of the swell should have assured some sense of calm, the surface of the water remained rough and choppy. He dropped his crawl and tried to find contentment in simply staying afloat. All around him, the ocean felt immense. He could have been ten years old again, hardly even a speck in the grand scheme of things. His teeth chattered loudly, though the worst of the cold had passed now that his body had begun to adjust to the bleak temperature, and he pulled breath in loud sodium-tinged rasps. The shore had come to seem very far away, a faint boomerang of grey pinned like a smothered sunrise between the immense black sheets of sky and ocean. The waves broke in similar shade, the ruptured crescents sparking flashes that bloomed and then were lost, devoured by the darkness.

Just as the rain began to fall, he was struck by a terrible thought. What if he were to drown? He was a long way from shore, in the sort of swell that would challenge even the most seasoned of swimmers. There had been a time, perhaps, when he could have managed in conditions like these, but he was in his forties now and hadn't been in the sea in years. He was out of his depth in every imaginable way. Panic sluiced through him with each forced breath, and every wave seemed to crash a little harder around his head and shoulders. If he drowned, what would people think? No doubt, he'd be labelled a suicide, and all the things that hung in such tenuous balance would suddenly make sense. He'd be missing for a full day or even two, maybe longer. It was, after all, November. For the first twenty-four hours, people would wonder about his whereabouts but almost certainly not act on their theories, not beyond a few cursory calls to known friends and then, when every other avenue of possibility had been exhausted, to the nearest hospital. Just in case there had been an accident. But as the time built, more serious questions would be asked, and at some point a search party would have to be organised. It might take days before anyone thought to turn their attention out to this small, sheltered stretch of beach. By then, the tides would have had their way with him, and there'd be no guarantee that his body would ever be found. A boat might get lucky, or he may become snagged on the rocks, but those things left a great deal to chance, and the odds were, at the best estimate, slender. But whoever did come looking out here would find traces of him, and the folded pile of his clothes, his priest's clothes, would strip away all doubt as to what had happened. They'd survey the situation and jump to the inevitable conclusion. Nobody would believe that he had simply got into trouble while swimming, because even though that was exactly what was happening, it made no sense. Men didn't get up in the middle of a cold, wet November night and simply decide to go for a dip. So they'd weigh up the ample evidence and chalk up a result of suicide.

He couldn't let that happen. Well, not without putting up a fight. The panic threatened to overwhelm him now, and he had to battle the urge to kick, knowing that, by doing so, he would waste energy in a hurry and that what little hope there was would be quickly lost. Instead, he continued to tread water and fought for calmness, forcing himself to draw a series of deep, steady breaths. The shoreline did seem a long way off, but when the next big wave hit he lunged forward and began to swim. His technique was inevitably poor, and he felt himself drift as currents rode across him and waves beat hard over his body, trying to force him under, but he kept his focus and stretched out, undeterred. It was clear that he had to use the tide, that fighting against its pull was a useless undertaking.

Twice, he was forced to stop in order to regain his strength, and by the second time he was so weak that it seemed the easiest option was just to close his eyes and let himself go under. There would be peace then, at least. All the problems would slip away, all the worries about what lay ahead for him in the weeks and months to come, times when there'd seem little difference between innocence and guilt and when facts hardly mattered at all. But sometimes it was not a question of coming down on one side of a choice, not when muscles fought and worked of their own accord, even when, drawn to the very brink of exhaustion, they were beginning to knot and cramp. The second time he stopped, he considered his distance from the beach and it was clear that he had gained considerable ground. Though he had a long way yet to go, some part of him was able to grasp onto this small hope and use it to force himself on.

Hours seemed to pass, and at times his arms felt so heavy that he didn't believe he could raise even one more stroke, but when he pushed his body there was always the strength for another, and another. He really might have been ten again, because all the unimportant things had been lost to the depths; but the difference was that, where it had been simply instinctive back then, he understood this now. Even if he failed to make it, he'd have taken this small but absolute knowledge from his life.

The sand that bit into his knees felt like a coarse lie. His hands tore channels in that sand and he was crawling. Rain fell in torrents, lashing his head and back, and a thin sound, like small screams, whistled through the clotted air. It was some minutes before he realised those screams were his, the noise of his lungs taken to the very brink and trying desperately to re-inflate. The ocean's spent waves washed foam around his knees, and sand clung to his flesh as he scrambled a little further up the beach, still crawling. Then, finally collapsing, he became one with the darkness.

He awoke to a vague cracked dawn. For a moment, he lay still, just staring up at the heavy sky. Clouds folded one across another, dull, angry shades of steel. He tried, finally, to raise his head, but could hardly muster the strength. His body had turned to stone, and every breath felt brushed with salt and something vaguely metallic. Wind blustered, tossing flecks of sand over his naked body. The strongest gusts drew howls where they sifted through the crevices of the rocks, tinny wails rising up out of flapping whimpers and just as quickly dying away, and they made him recall the old stories of the Banshee. Was that all it had ever been, he wondered, just the wind sluicing through trees or out-croppings of rock? Or had it once been something more?

He knew that he had survived certain drowning, surely a miracle, but he couldn't find even a stirring of happiness in the fact. In his mind, it made God cruel beyond compare for saving him. His experience had been that problems rarely found their own solutions, and the life that spun ahead of him seemed set to offer only pain: a circus of accusations, maybe even the horrifying indignity of a trial. It was hard to locate even a grain of compassion in sparing him for that sort of ordeal. Mercy, real mercy, would have been to drag him under without giving him the chance to think his way out of what was happening. This, he knew, was what people meant when they spoke of having their very own crosses to bear. Sick with anger, he lay back, studied the sky and cursed the heavens.

There was a solution, of course. All he had to do was wade back out into the water, out and out until he was deep enough to sink. But where, just a few hours ago, the idea of a swim thrilled every nerve in his body, now the prospect of that coldness was too much to even contemplate. The edge of the sea lay some twenty feet or so away, caught in mid-retreat, and the surface moiled with a vicious cunning. God was at it again, talking him out of his bad thoughts.

After an hour, he got slowly to his feet and staggered up the beach to where he had left his clothes. They were wet through and coated in sand. He thought of taking them down to the water's edge and rinsing them out, but the idea seemed to call for too much energy. He dressed, not caring about how the clothes felt around him, then considered the ocean once more. It was as restless as before, the waves churning their whitish bilge up against the strand. Finally, he turned and walked up the beach to where he had dropped his bicycle.

FIT FOR A HIGH KING

Sunday was the day he set aside for tending to the grass. Every Sunday morning, after first mass had ended, he'd climb the low hill behind the chapel to where the graveyard lay hunched against the wind. The passing years had made the whole thing less of a chore, somehow, and there were midweek days now when he'd straighten up from the handle of the plough, groaning as some invisible hammer beat painful nails into his lower lumbar region, and find himself thinking almost wistfully of the Sunday to come, that hour or two that he'd spend on his knees over the grave, scraping moss and the stubbornly creeping fronds of ivy from the granite headstone, tearing weeds and dandelions from the stone trimming, and keeping the grass low and uniform with a pair of small hand-shears. Some of the graves, the newer ones, had coloured pebbles, chippings that shone like stained glass whenever it rained, but he was determined that his grave should have grass.

He had never married. He knew that many people in the village thought him odd, a little bit eccentric, but some men just weren't the type who bothered with such details as wives and families. Early on that had bothered him a little, and there were plenty of nights coming in cold and weary from the fields when he could have imagined nothing nicer in the world than the idea of a wife waiting to comfort him with a few gentle words. Other men returned home on such nights to a smiling woman, to the enticing smell of a lamb stew, the promise of a roaring fire and a comfortable chair. And in bed, maybe a late embrace, some small but heartfelt human contact that could make a lot of things seem better than they really were. His lot, though, was to open his door to a cold breeze and darkness. Occasionally, out of some determination, he'd find half an hour during the day to prepare a pot of stew, and he'd make enough then to last a week or more, piling every ingredient that came to hand into a large pot and letting the whole concoction simmer until everything – the cheapest cuts of mutton or beef as well as the carrots and potatoes and onions and pearl barley, even cabbage, if he had it – had been reduced down to something like a gelatinous pulp. Later, and in the nights that followed, he'd eat plates of the stuff out of duty and because it offered a modicum of heat, and he'd sneer at the empty fireplace and tell himself that he didn't need a wife, that it wouldn't be worth having a woman around just for the sake of a pot of stew. Women were peculiar sorts. He recalled his mother, but vaguely; she had been as peculiar as any of them, fussing over things that didn't matter at all, moaning about never having enough money, or needing a new dress, or about the condition of the wallpaper. The kind of complaints that, if truth be told, really had very little to do with living. And he remembered, too, how his father would stand there, head bowed until his stubble-ridden chin was planted against his chest, kneading the top rung of a kitchen chair's back, those big hard hands fairly strangling the wood. His father had been a strong man in almost every way imaginable, but when women talked, there was nothing to be said.

Some men needed wives, just as some needed to be told when to wake up, when to eat and how to dress. Others got by just fine on their own, and if the solitude of that could be lonesome, it could also be soothing. It was true that he hadn't set out intentionally to remain alone, and back in his younger days he could cast his eye with the best of them, but as he left behind his twenties and wandered on into an imperceptibly deep middle-age, he found that living alone was a state that suited him just fine. In his life, there was no one to complain when he drank too much, no one to push him to mend broken things around the house or to paint walls that would only grow dirty again anyway from the smoke of the turf fire. He used the house for eating and sleeping, nothing more than that, and over the years his personality had developed too many sharp corners to bother much about comforts and soft things.

Money was his way of measuring success. After his father died, the farm had come to him. It was in a shambling state, rundown and barely viable, but he worked hard to make a go of things, tending to the major problems first and then slowly extending until eventually he had doubled their landholding to almost thirty acres, rearing herds of upwards of eighty head of cattle. After a time, it no longer even felt like work to him. He'd rise at four, toil in the fields or in the barns until nine or ten o'clock at night, and even later in the summer, until he knew every blade of grass and pothole on his land, every hair on the back of every cow. As a small personal indulgence, he kept an acre free for growing potatoes and cabbages, and he tended to that patch of ground like a devout gardener. Beyond that, there was little else he needed.

The idea of a grave struck him one day while he was furrowing the ground to lay a row of spring onions. His years of hard work had paid off, making him a wealthy man, and while his hands cut open the dark soil he let his mind wander as to what sort of things people spent money on in their search for happiness. He was aware that some men liked to throw away their hard-earned savings on fine cars, noisy low-slung Italian things that were painted in the gaudiest of colours and could cover a hundred miles of distance in a faster time than it took a thirsty man to put away a pint of stout. Others squandered what they earned on trips abroad, to all those places that looked cut out of a John Wayne film or a wildlife programme. But he already had a van, an old rust-laden shell of a thing that couldn't boast much in the way of engine-might but which got him – with just a little coaxing – where he wanted or needed to go. And he didn't see himself as much of a one for holidays, either. The farm needed him here, not wandering around Hollywood or Kenya or the Grand Canyon. But he had enough money hoarded now, probably more than he'd ever need, and he had the idea that he'd really like to buy himself something nice, something that would feel sufficiently rewarding for all those years of slavery to the farm. He just couldn't decide what that might be.

And then the idea stormed his mind.

It felt so complete and perfect that he raised himself from his knees and pushed his filthy hands into the small of his back, his face tilted towards the sun. The sky wasn't much to look at; clouds of veined marble, bruised and headed with the assurance of a springtime outburst, and the small yellow sun seemed as mediocre as ever, a glowing thumbprint of little worth. The idea boomed through his mind with all the sung hosannas of a revelation, but the world around him looked unperturbed. He'd been searching for something more than mere flash, something that would last longer than a memory or a well-maintained motor. Something with the eternal qualities of rock, if such a thing were possible. And there it was, fully conceived in his mind's eye: a grave. And not just any grave either, but the biggest and very best grave in the parish, maybe even the county. That was perfect. All other considerations fell away and he set himself to planning.

He paid out for a pocket-sized hardbound notebook and a good pen. Organisation, he decided, was probably the key to a successful hunt. And every Sunday after first mass, instead of getting himself back to the chores that were stacking up around the farm, he took himself on tours of local villages to spend an hour or so just strolling around their graveyards. The Protestant graves, on the whole, tended to be more impressive than their Catholic counterparts, and after a few weeks he gave up on the Catholic graveyards altogether. He was fifty-two years old and, while time wasn't necessarily of the essence, he decided that there was no sense in being wasteful about it either. Focus was important.

Within a month he was forced to widen his search, and his Sunday excursions became all-day affairs, carrying him further and further afield until he was fringing the county bounds, wading through knee-high swathes of nettles and dogweed and poking around in jungles of collapsing headstones. Afterwards, he'd lunch in one pub or another, taking on board a pint of stout and a sandwich if there was one to be had, really making a day of it. He'd settle in the corner snug, relax with his pint and set to scribbling down descriptions of what he had seen. The notebook filled steadily, to the point where he had to buy a second one, and in this he broke his explorations down into categories that compared height, width and stone type. Such behaviour didn't seem obsessive, no more obsessive surely than the way some men hoarded the statistics of their favourite hurling teams. He'd found himself a hobby, that was all, and an enjoyable one, at that. And though many of the stones he looked at were rubbed bare by exposure to decades, even centuries, of rain and gale, he developed a fondness for inscriptions that were pithy or poetic, and he noted the best ones down with care, not so much with the intention of utilising them for his own epitaph, but simply for personal pleasure. Near the back of the second notebook were crude but generally successful sketches of the very best stones, the towering Celtic crosses and trumpeting cherubs. One grave he'd seen had even carried the very shape of Death itself, a hooded figure armed with a scythe. Time had broken away the points and edges, but the menace was no less fearsome for that, and even though he shivered at the notion of having such a sculpture loom above him for all eternity, there was something sort of enticing about it, too.

Eventually, after he had exhausted virtually every graveyard of note in the entire county, he turned his thoughts to making a decision. Granite seemed the logical choice of stone. Marble was strong, yes, but its lacquered gleam felt overpowering, not in keeping with his idea of eternal rest. He liked old, unfussy things, and marble just felt too contemporary. Granite had no patina; it could be cut smooth and polished clean but it would still hold the sense of having been hauled from the earth.

Both of his parents lay in the family plot, a double grave set in the upper tier of the cemetery. The first Sunday after early mass that he had taken himself up there, he grimaced with shame. It was his first visit in years. Christ, how long was it? Twenty? More than that, he decided. He stood shin-deep in weeds and briars, and bowed his head. The headstone that had stood since the time of his great-grandfather on his father's side, a short and simple stone cross that even in his childhood had long since been worn clean of markings, now lay knocked over backwards and smashed into three distinct pieces. The ocean gales and violent rainfall had done for it, he knew, that incessant natural beat pounding until it had shifted and reshaped the very earth itself. He drew and spent a deep, weary breath. The morning was overcast, the hillside draped in a thin veil of mist. A hunchbacked willow tree leaned down from behind the cemetery's nearby boundary wall, its leaves shifting and soughing in the cold air. He should never have allowed his family grave to deteriorate so badly, but the farm had eaten up years of his life, and time had passed so quickly.

He turned, just before starting back down the hillside, and considered his surround. The village stretched away down below; he could make out familiar buildings, and he could see where the sweep and rise of the land cloaked his farm from sight. In the west, the ocean rolled, a torpid grey slate flecked with frothing, breeze-tugged spumes. But up here, everything felt calm and peaceful, the mist and the feral edge of dishevelment adding something elemental to the atmosphere. A sense of the eternal, he decided.

Things needed to be put to rights. Every Sunday morning, he made the slow climb, doing a little at a time. For a man so used to the rigours of manual labour, it would have been easily within his capabilities to clear the site in two or three visits, but he had no reason to hurry, and the routine became so quickly and easily pleasurable that he would have happily toiled at the chore forever, weeding, plucking stones, turning the earth and trimming the grass. Every week, mindless of the weather, he'd limit himself to an hour or two of work. Afterwards, he'd take himself down to Reilly's pub in the village, and he'd sit at the end of the bar, or by the fire once the days began to take on a chill that made it all the way into his bones. And once the stout had taken full hold, he'd profess aloud, though to no one in particular, that there was not a grave in the village, even in the entire county, that could compare with his own. 'Once the stone is in place, you'll all see what I mean,' he'd gasp, because the drink had a habit these days of making him slightly breathless. 'Fit for a High King,' he'd add, letting the worn stubs of his dirt-encrusted fingers push the scattering of loose coins around the table, enough for one more pint, perhaps two. It was difficult to break old habits; money was a hard-earned thing, to be equated with exhaustion, sore hands and back pain, and the idea of parting so freely with it, especially on such a frivolous indulgence as drink, jarred with him. So one more, maybe two, and that would have to be his lot. 'Fit for a High King,' he'd say, and some of the other men at the bar or seated nearby would look up and nod. By then, though, most had heard it all before. They'd tend to their own pints and let him talk until he'd drank away his coins or until his sense had returned. Then he'd rise, nod goodbye to old Reilly behind the bar, and make his way home to put in the few hours of remaining daylight at baling hay, milking the goat, or tending to any one of a hundred other small demands insisted upon by his little piece of farm.

The sculptors refused to etch his name into the stone. He tried to explain what he wanted, that of course they'd have to leave the date blank but the rest could be worked on, surely, the names of those gone before him and, at the bottom, his own name. They agreed to everything, even the leading epitaph on which he had settled: 'The Dineen family', and just below, in a beautiful Old English script, 'They worked the soil'. But when it came to adding his own name, he was met with outright refusal. Some legal grey area, apparently. 'Anyway, don't you think that's a bit on the ghoulish side?' the man on the telephone had said, in a tone that seemed obtuse and not a little judgemental, and there was nothing else to do but give in, because there was just no talking to some people. Besides, once the stone was in the ground even the law would find it pretty difficult to stop him adding anything he wished. And surely there was more than one man in Cork that could handle a chisel.

He had gone to the showrooms to select the type of stone he wanted, had driven all the way up to Charleville on a workday in order to spend over an hour with one of their salesmen, James, a tall, pallid young man who led him smoothly through their extensive catalogue of designs while they drank cup after cup of hot sweet tea. When it was clear that he meant business, that he was here to spend some significant money, nothing seemed too much trouble. The young salesman had the receptionist run out for sandwiches and freshly baked scones, and yet more tea was served. The Celtic cross was indeed a classic design, James assured him. Distinguished and impressive. And of course it could be made to hold in even the most yielding of ground; that was merely a question of counterpoint. One of their best men would survey the site, every aspect would be given the fullest consideration, and a necessary foundation stone would be arranged. 'Have no worries at all on that score,' the young man said, flashing a practised smile.

Outside the large plate glass window of the showroom, a stiff easterly wind had brought nubs of sleet into the late morning, but here inside it felt bright and warm. The soft tanned leather chairs were comfortable enough to sleep in, and the tea and scones tasted very good indeed. In the end, it came down to a choice between a pair of plump-looking angels hovering above a large slab of open book, and the tallest and most ornate of their crosses. They only had a mid-sized cross in stock, a grand looking piece of work of essentially the same design, and while the angels did look impressive, if anything maybe even more impressive given some of the minute details, the cross just seemed right somehow.

He stood beside it, traced a hand gently over the carefully sculpted surface to feel the ripples of some ancient scrolled pattern, and nodded. 'I like it,' he said, but what he liked even more was that, since they had no fit model in stock, one would have to be created from scratch, and just for him. 'I'm afraid that you can probably expect to wait upwards of six months,' the salesman said, 'but there is an added bonus, so to speak, in that I can show you some samples of Celtic inlay patterns and you can choose one to your very own specifications.' A large plain base-stone would carry the engraved details, names and dates and so forth, and a blank strip slightly above mid-point on the cross, set about chest-height and raised slightly from the intricately woven stem, would bear the requested epitaph. A twenty per cent deposit was required up front, and he stared hard at the young man for seconds that began to stretch uncomfortably towards a minute before clearing his throat and nodding. 'I suppose,' he muttered, then withdrew a roll of notes from the inside pocket of his coat and with the greatest of reluctance began to count them out.

After that, it was simply a matter of waiting. Well, time wasn't a problem, and there were plenty of ways to make it pass, not least with work. The farm always needed something doing, but he still made the pilgrimage up the hill to the graveyard every Sunday after mass, and even through the family grave was now in pristine condition, he still found a few weeds to pull, still trimmed the grass with his shears and tended to the trim. Mostly, though, he liked to sit up there, settling down on a small boulder that could not have been more convenient if it had been placed there by hand, and he'd fold his arms against the cold, sink down into his overcoat and imagine how splendid the grave would look when the stone was finally in place. The village spread itself out below, quiet in its day of rest, now that the worshippers had dispersed, and the harbour was quiet too, the few tethered rowboats rocking on the tide, the anchored fishing boats drifting out against their line and slowly back again with the roll of the sea. He couldn't help but wonder whether or not the cross would be visible from down there. His family's grave was right on the cusp of the hill where the land flattened out, and he felt certain that from the low perspective of the pier or the main street the cross would rise proud and tall against the skyline, emphasised by the muted shifting of the clouds.

In February, he was taken ill. At first, it seemed nothing serious, a touch of that flu that was doing the rounds. He had a high fever and a numbing ache in his joints, but everyone knew that there was nothing for flu but to stay in bed. The farm would have to survive without him, he decided, when he tried to rise that second morning only to find that his legs would not bear his weight. He gave in to the wave of lethargy that swept over him, slumped back into bed and slept through the dawn for the first time in his adult life. When he finally woke it was almost noon and, convincing himself that he was feeling better, he struggled into his clothes and went to sit at the kitchen table. The little food he managed to eat, two slices of bread and some grated cheddar, made him nauseous, but the whiskey that he sipped did seem to help, at least for a while. Then he slept again, this time in the armchair beside the bare fireplace, wrapped up in his overcoat and an old wool blanket to keep out the bitter cold of the house, and it was all most unlike him, really.

The following day he made two telephone calls. For a long time he had resisted the notion of a telephone in the house, but now he was glad of the contraption. The first call went to Kelleher, a request, posed as a favour, to send one of the young lads down to look after things, the cattle mainly, just for a few days. A fee was suggested and agreed upon without argument, and Kelleher, who had always been a scrupulously fair man in his dealings, business or otherwise, was no less so now. He thanked his neighbour, put down the receiver so that he could give in to the coughing fit that was tugging at his breath, and then he dialled again, this time putting a call through to Dr Lenihan.

Lenihan, a man in his sixties with a long narrow face, mournful green eyes and pale, almost translucent flesh, arrived a little after six. 'It's the flu,' he said with a shrug, after performing a quick examination. 'You'll live, I dare say, though it might take a week or even two before you're back to anything like your old self again.' Smiling didn't become him, it looked sordid somehow, but he only gave it a moment on the surface before bottling it up again for the next patient. 'Here,' he added, just before leaving. 'Let me write you out a prescription to see if we can't shift that cough of yours.' Then he took his money and was gone. The whole area was enduring something of an epidemic, and he was far too busy to waste time on idle chatter.

The week dragged. Every morning, Dineen woke from a restless night expecting to feel better, even a little better. And every morning he was disappointed. The cough was still there, a stabbing thing now that pecked away at his chest and which made it hurt to swallow, and he had no strength at all left in his body. He lay in bed, drifting in and out of his dreams and wishing away the days and, even more so, the nights, suffering his share and then some. Then, on the ninth or tenth morning, he staggered to the bathroom on trembling legs and moaned, eyes clenched shut, as he passed blood. Terror flushed through him and he crumpled to the floor. Kelleher's eldest, Michael, found him a couple of hours later. Over the past days, the boy had fallen into a routine of stopping by the house on his way from one chore to the next, just to see that everything was okay and to give an assurance that the cattle were fine, that the farm was in safe hands. By nightfall, Dineen was in a hospital bed and a battery of tests, bloods, scans, x-rays, begun. The cancer, though, had spread too far and was beyond treatment. The best they could do said the solemn-faced doctors and the pretty but slightly disconnected nurses, was to make him comfortable, to keep his pain at bay. Palliative care, they called it, a big word for something that he couldn't even begin to understand.

On St Patrick's Day, Kelleher came to visit and from under his coat produced a flask of whiskey. 'What do you say we wet the shamrock, boy?' he said, and the nurse, who fully understood the situation, cleared her throat in a not-quite-disapproving manner, produced two water glasses and muttered something around a smirk about not having seen a thing. Dineen accepted a drop, but could do no more than take the spirit on his tongue. Swallowing was too much for him. Then he lowered the glass and nodded occasionally to his visitor's efforts at small-talk. There was no mention of what would happen to the land and the cattle, because this was neither the time nor the place, but also because the high doses of medication made him mentally unfit for such a discussion. Under the influence of such potent drugs, all he wanted to talk about was his new headstone. It would arrive at the beginning of the summer, he said, a beautiful Celtic cross, hand-sculpted to order, and it would be the finest stone in the entire county.

Kelleher was familiar with the details, just like everyone else in the village, but rather than let his impatience show he smiled and nodded his head and said that yes, it would surely be something to see, all right. Fit for a High King, indeed. And when Dineen began to struggle against the pull of sleep, he got to his feet and said that, well, he'd better be getting back, that there were a hundred things to be done before night, but that he'd call again, soon. A promise. 'Don't worry about any-thing except getting better,' he said, and he'd remember those words often in the months to come, knowing that they were the last words his old neighbour had ever heard from anyone who was not a doctor or a nurse or a priest.

A fortnight to the day, the hearse arrived in the village. The weather was fine for early April, cold but bright and dry, and just about everyone in the locality turned out for the funeral, filed into the little chapel and then afterwards stood around the opened grave and said that it was a real shock, him having never been sick a day in his life that anyone could recall. And a crying shame, too, that he'd left no one behind to mourn his loss. Especially with him being such a wealthy man. Just about the only mercy that could be said about the whole business was that it had been quick in the end, hardly more than a couple of months from start to finish.

The Celtic cross had yet to arrive, but that hardly seemed so important now. That was a detail, nothing more, a material possession designed purely to shore up the ego; time would put that matter right, just as time would eventually wear it down to dust. Besides, it wasn't hulking headstones that made high kings, or even that preserved the memory of them. Only stories did that, tales that turned history to fancy. And down there in the musky and slightly fetid earth all became one, the high king and the farmer, levelled at last, dust to dust, one inseparable from the other. Stories were what mattered most, then.

The priest rumbled through the duties of prayer while the gathered crowd breathed the clean, sea-blown air of the hillside, and wandering eyes watched the breakers rip open the tide out in the harbour, just for something on which to focus their attention. Then, with the formalities complete, they picked their steps along the muddy path out through the rusted, leaning wing of gate and on down to the village, the women turning for home, most of the men slipping in to Reilly's pub so that they might take the harshness out of their thirsts and bury the man properly.

REVELATIONS

I saw my exact double in Manhattan, walking down Fourth
Avenue. Honestly. And in my mind I can still see him
now, as clear as any reflection. He is clean shaven except
for a ropy piece of moustache with tails that hang all the
way down his chin, and he wears a dark grey pinstripe suit
that is probably a long train ride out of my league. His
whole image – the moustache and the suit, but other things
too, tiny details that combine to create this air of strict,
cultivated perfection – looks more trouble than it is worth,
but surface foibles aside, it really could be myself that I am
seeing. There are things going on in the world that we can't
even begin to comprehend.

The experience bothers me, I can't pretend otherwise.
As soon as I get back to the hotel, I put a call through to
my wife. While I wait for the fuzz to clear and that tinny
bell sound to stop, my eyes scan the wall of the phone box.
Booths, they call them over here. The cork is littered with
scribbled words and numbers, such a crisscrossed score of
blue, black and red-penned graffiti that the messages lose

any value they might once have contained. It takes me a moment to realise that I am searching for dirty words; my tongue plays against my palate to make a small, disapproving tut sound, then I blow it away with a sigh. I suppose I'd been hoping for a limerick, and I'm probably in need of the amusement. A mad fluttering has made a shaken cocktail of my insides. I really can't get over just how much this fellow looked like me.

Through the receiver's earpiece the clanging ring-tone notes push on with determination, a steady stacking, but I am too upset and anxious to keep count. The fluttering inside of me is severe, a quiver that must surely be visible. In this imagining sort of mood I get to thinking about cartoons, chiefly Sylvester and Tweety. On the very few occasions that the cat did manage to catch his supper, little old Tweety Pie would just kick up a fuss, flapping and pecking, until there was nothing left for Sylvester to do but open up that mouth in abject surrender. That's how I feel now, standing in the phone box and pressing my sweaty ear against the receiver. Well, sort of, anyway. But when I try that cure, opening up my mouth, I find no relief. The bird in my stomach is having far too much fun churning my insides to butter. Waiting here at the receiver isn't easy – patience has never been one of my virtues – but today I think I am prepared to wait all day long, if that is what it takes. I'm after peace of mind, and maybe the succour of a friendly voice. Just now, those things take on the mantle of gold and uncut diamonds, treasures unbound. And finally, on perhaps the twentieth or twenty-fourth ring, the call connects. There is a moment of fumbling, chunky crackling sounds that remind me of other things from other times, and then, at last, the breathy hello that opens up my smile.

'Jen? It's me.'

'Sean? Is something wrong? Are you okay?'

I can feel her confusion, and for a moment it confuses me. There is a fogged texture to her voice, as if she is speaking through a veil. She doesn't seem to be breathing right, too hoarse. I clear my throat, but it doesn't help. Technology really is a wonder, though. Imagine, an ocean and a mass of land stands between us, thousands of miles of busy people and salt water soughing back and forth, stretches of calm, more stretches still buffeted by raging storms. And yet, here we are, talking. Okay, so she's not clear as a day or anything – those miles have to count for something – but it isn't anywhere near so bad that I can't make out her words. I suppose it is the same at her end. We might as well be a room away from one another, muffled only by a wall instead of half a world.

'Listen, Jen. There's something I need to tell you. Now, I know that this will probably sound like I've dropped my bag of marbles, but I think it's important.' She knows of my belief in anything even vaguely supernatural, knows that I have always held such fancies as omens and premonitions in the very highest esteem, and she can probably read by the way I groan a preparatory breath that I am about to deliver some newfound thesis of my latest life trauma. I wait for some feedback, but there is nothing from her end at all but the dust-filled static of her waiting, and all I can do is push on. 'I saw myself, Jen,' I say, taking things slowly. This is long-distance, after all. Plenty of room for confusion. 'Not an hour ago. I swear to God, just walking down the street. I was dressed differently, and I'd lost the beard for something a bit more stylish, but it was absolutely me.' I want to say more, to paint pictures for her if I can, but the words pile up against a hard reflex swallow and I find myself waiting for her response. That's probably best; I am excited and upset, always a Toad's Wild Ride combination where I am concerned. I wish that I could explain myself a little better, but even at the best of times clarity is rarely my friend, so for now, what I've said will have to suffice.

What follows is a moment of total emptiness, echoes of nothing that roll along the line, gathering speed over thousands of travelled miles. Then they hit, jabbing into my head with all the force of a sonic boom, but silent. I am reeling when Jenny takes aim.

'What the hell is wrong with you, Sean?' She's not quite shouting, which is worse than shouting, a state she preserves for the most flaming of her rages. Shouting expends energy that can be better utilised in other ways. I can picture her very clearly, her mouth a wavy pencil line, her body all small and pent-up, sparking like a cut cable, fairly spitting with anger. I hold the belief that a day will come when she'll actually physically explode, just spontaneously combust. They say that such a thing happens and that it is a mystery as to why, but it is no mystery to me. Some people are calm by nature while others simmer until they simply boil over. Jenny is a volcano; she generates enormous inner heat. That can be an incredible thing at times, if you know what I mean, but mostly it terrifies me.

'It's the middle of the night, for Christ's sake.' That wavy mouth flaps for air with an audible slurping sound, but the words knot and tangle up inside her. She's as Irish as mutton stew and thatched cottages, and if her job has influenced her into acting like a modern woman and speaking with all slow, careful propriety, she still sings with a soft and lovely Galway brogue, and still blisters at a moment's notice to Civil War talk, her patriotism worn like a second layer of skin and her truest hide. But in moments of raw anger there is an undeniable Slavic bent to her make-up, a gypsy grounding that makes her gag with a plethora of ancient fire-breathing hexes and knife-wielding aggression. Seven years of marriage, of the tightest imaginable binds, have made me sensitive to even the slightest warning signs. My heart offers up a prayer of thanksgiving for the mercy of that ocean between us. 'You've been drinking. Come on, admit it. You have, haven't you?'

'No, I …'

'After the last time, you promised that you were done with it. "Never again," you said. Swore on your mother's soul that you'd stop.' Her bitter laugh sounds like a saw's blade chewing through wet oak. Dogs run from that laugh, coma patients shiver in their beds. 'And then, as soon as you get a step out of my sight, you're right back to your old ways.'

'Jen, I haven't been drinking. Honest to God. Just a glass of wine with lunch, and that was it.'

'Yeah,' she snarled. 'And the rest.'

'No, I mean it. Just a glass. Look, I swear, cross my heart and hope to die, stick a needle in my eye.' But she isn't in a laughing mood, and I really don't want to be giving her any ideas. 'Well, actually it was two half glasses, but that only adds up to one, doesn't it? And anyway, you know that wine doesn't do a thing to me.' Which is true; with whiskey I'm a devil and even beer can produce some unusual side-effects, but I could drink wine for a week straight and I wouldn't so much as stagger. I think I have an immunity to grapes and all their enemy variants.

Her breathing whistles with nasal alarm, and I have the thought that a dragon's menace is at least half its power. The worst of her rage has died away, but she likes her simmering anger, enjoys the sense of it around her slim frame, and she is predictably slow in letting that fully go. 'So, what the hell is so important that has you calling me up in the middle of the night? Damn near shifted the heart and soul inside of me, too. I mean, Christ, you really could be the world's heavyweight champion of selfish, stupid bastards, Sean Lenihan.'

'Is it the middle of the night?' I ask, pleading innocence but actually realising that I probably already know it. Japan is a long way away, and those time zones can pile up fast over water. 'I'm sorry, Jen. Really, I am. It's just, well, this thing has got me all turned around. I suppose I lost track of myself. You know how it is, I must have stopped thinking for a minute.'

'A minute? Your problem, Sean, is that you never think, or never think about anything or anyone else but yourself. Be honest now, you don't give a shit that you called me up at, what, nearly five o'clock in the morning? Just to tell me that you've seen someone who looked a little bit like you on the street. Well, here's a newsflash that might just shake you out of your little fucking centre-of-the-universe ego-trip: there are millions of people in New York, and there can be only so many faces to go round.'

She has said a mouthful, maybe more than she's intended to say. I can feel each word as a nail hammered into the bones of my chest, and through the phone-box's perspex window my stunned gaze watches the hotel lobby receive a heavy wash of clear white light. Rain on its way; we get that sort of light a lot where I live.

'What do you mean?' I say, trying hard not to whisper. What she gets is a croak, the best I've got.

'I mean, you really are a conceited son of a bitch. Christ almighty, Sean ...'

'No, not that.' We're past my imperfect state; I have already accepted my flaws as factual. 'What you said about faces.'

Her answer is a sigh. I take the air of it, almost feeling its slow weariness. 'I'm hanging up now, okay? I'll have to be up in another hour or so anyway, I've got a lecture to give at ten. Call me tonight, okay? Say about eight? Whatever time that is over there.'

I think I catch a hint of thawing. But just a hint. We've been married long enough now for me to be able to recognise the signs, I suppose. Seven years, a long time since she'd swept me off my feet. To be honest, that whole corner of my life is like a blur to me now, like something safely interred behind a mass of concrete in an effort to benefit my health. We met at the afters of a wedding, some friend-of-a-friend gathering that looked to me like a convenient excuse for some serious drinking. I was coming off the ropes of a relationship gone sour and had spent the past couple of months or so just limping from one black hole of a bar to the next. It had been that or else cry myself to sleep every night, and I needed the liquid. Jen came dancing across the floor, swept on a wind of 'Just The Way You Are', the wedding singer tottering a couple of tones too high for comfort and fathoms of the food-chain removed from Billy Joel. If I had been sober I'd probably be still laughing now, all these years later: Jen had moves that were far too old-fashioned for a twenty-four-year-old. People who can't dance should stay off dance floors, just as people who can't drive have no business behind the wheel of a car. But I suppose there are times in our lives when we all have to make do with what we've got. And hours of dedication at the bar had made me less judgemental. She looked good in blue and with her hair up, and when her eyes fixed on me her man-hungry smile widened to show incisors. I was feeling like I had been dropkicked off the back of a speeding bus, my heart held together with band-aids and blue tack, so I was a famished dog for the least crumb of female affection. I'm certain that we looked a right pair as we twisted or jived our unsteady way first through the usual wedding fare of 'Do You Want To Dance', 'All My Loving' and something with a strong Bo Diddley beat that I can still feel in my heart and in my feet even to this day, but which I have never been able to identify. After some kind of eternal struggle we made it through to something slower, 'Wonderful Tonight' and then 'Smoke Gets In Your Eyes'. As I've said, she was no great mover, but she learned right off that I couldn't dance either; whenever I felt myself wilting or running out of steps, I simply slipped into robot mode.

A robot whose hinges needed oiling. A lot of girls would have started running right there and then, because dancing wasn't the half of it, really, when it came to inventorying the things I couldn't do, but in Jenny's family twenty-four was practically old maid status, so running probably wasn't at the top of her list of options that night. And the rest, as they say, is history, filler for some boring book.

'Happy' is a heavyweight word, similar to 'love' in certain respects. I'm not sure that our life together has been heavyweight enough to deserve such a label, but we are okay. When you can pass the days without despising the very sight of one another, you can get by. There are plenty of people worse off than us, and that's a fact. We both work hard, and we've built up a comfortable sort of existence – a nice house, two cars that even on cold mornings start without too much coaxing. No kids have entered our little equation yet and we have no plans for any, at least not in our immediate future. It's not that we've been actively preventing them, but we haven't really been trying either. We communicate about small things, the busy nothings of bills and holidays and what colours to decorate the living-room this summer. The bigger issues are left to take care of themselves and, for the most part, they do. We have our moments, of course, like all couples, but our arguments tend to blow themselves out quickly, like kindling fire. In arguments, I just bow my head. I tell myself that it is because I don't want to fuel Jen's flames, but the truth is that I prefer peace to war, even if it means abject surrender. Jenny rages with blitzkrieg force, trampling my meagre defences. I let her have her way, because it doesn't matter so much to me.

I'm in New York to meet some buyers. I work for an electronics firm, American-owned, Irish-based. I know nothing about the inner turmoil of our products beyond what I have learned by heart from crib-sheets, all that scientific jargon as gibberish to my mind as the workings of a human heart or a long-lost tribal language, but for some reason I have become quite a successful sales rep, or successful by my own apathetic standards. Jen says that it probably has something to do with the fact that I don't come across as pushy. It is true that a lot of salesmen take a Nazi approach to moving product, all aggressive muscle-flexing and overpowering spiel. My buyers consider my offer and then find themselves leaning in to ask for my own opinion, as if I am a close and trusted friend. Even people I've met for the first time just an hour before tend to pick up on some peculiar but sating vibe. They instinctively understand that I am not out to con them. Maybe they see that I don't really care whether they buy or not. Jen says that my beard makes me look a little like a cocker spaniel. I've never been able to make that connection, but perhaps she is on to something. People, generally, are fond of dogs. Whatever the reasons, I'm surprisingly good at the work I do, though I could just as soon be working at digging ditches or painting walls. For the past couple of years, all the talk on the factory floor has been that the company is on the verge of closing down their Irish operation and moving lock, stock and barrel to Asia. Over there, they can produce the goods at a fraction of the price, apparently. Well, business is all about profit margins, but I've stopped worrying. They'll do what's best for them, and I can do without the grief of yet another stomach ulcer.

New York is a city that appeals to me. There are a few others around the world that I enjoy, but New York is high on my list of favourites. I love the claustrophobia of the streets, the vibrancy of packed sidewalks and traffic jams. Where I come from we don't have buildings like these. On this particular occasion, I find myself here for a week, but I have made this trip several times before and the routine of my visits rarely deviates. My business can usually be managed by late morning and culminates in an expenses-covered lunch at some exorbitantly overpriced bistro that leaves you soul-hungry even after three immaculately designed courses. The buyers eat and drink, and Asian, African or American, they smile a lot and ask me questions about Ireland that have nothing at all to do with the matter at hand. I tell them about the joys of lake-fishing and what the weather is like, advise them on the best time of year to visit and the places and sights that really should be seen. These men – they are almost always men – are uniformly middle-aged, balding, overweight and weary-looking in a thick-boned way. They are my own future set in fleshy stone, unless I shake up my destiny. I listen as they talk with enthusiasm about things like Guinness and Irish music, and some of them can even quote a few lines of Yeats, perhaps 'The Lake Isle of Innisfree' or 'The Song of Wandering Aengus'. And to a man they insist that they'll be making that trip shortly, next year probably, or the year after for certain, but I know that they'll never visit. It does no harm to dream, as long as you don't take it too much to heart. After lunch, we stand and shake hands, and the deal is closed in word-of-mouth assurance, only the details remaining to be tied up at the paperwork stage that is the lawyers' domain. We shake hands and they drift away, feeling with a delirious tinge of embarrassment that they have just forged a new friendship, leaving me free with the rest of the day to be filled as I choose. A week of afternoons to be spent wandering around Greenwich Village trying to imagine how it must have been for Bob Dylan and Dylan Thomas, or sipping an espresso at the red-and-white check-patterned street-side table of some restaurant in shrinking Little Italy. I enjoy the colours and the noise of Chinatown, and spinning back and forth across the Hudson on the Staten Island ferry, leaning against the railing and filling up with the view of a sun-drenched skyline. The Statue of Liberty looks smaller than I had always imagined, and each time I see it I feel a quiver of surprise. You'd think that by now my expectations would have reined themselves in, but there it is, that same quiver of surprise, every single time. And by the first fall of darkness, I have worked up a sizeable thirst.

At the moment, Jenny is also away from home. She works as a research assistant to a noted pharmacology professor, a crusty old letch named Alsop who, some years ago, gained certain recognition in the field by happening across one of those rare and precious eureka moments. The idea, whatever it was, saw him lauded with the sort of honour that has ever since put him in great demand on the lecturing circuit, and he is currently fixed to a three-month visiting tenure at Hokkaido University, teaching some new theory of pharmacokinetics. So it is that Jen, as an integral part of his team, a staff of four who clamour to fulfil his every scientific whim, finds herself there, too. Well, she's always had a travelling bone and there may be some truth in the old saying about absence making the heart grow fonder. 'Which fonder?' I always say, when she brings that up. 'You can have Peter if you want him, but give me Jane any day.' I always had a thing for Barbarella. We've made it this far though, seven years, so she might have a point.

Jenny says that this new stuff, this latest pharmacokinetics angle, is either crackpot or brilliant, but that as it is still only at the strictly theoretical stage it may take years before anyone can pass a definitive judgement one way or the other. That's nice work if you can get it. I've met Alsop a few times, but have never been able to warm to the man. His pale, hyperthyroid eyes seem to dart everywhere, and his tiny red mouth is scarred with a perpetual and very unsettling smile. When that smile widens a little into laughter, he shows off the smallest teeth that I have ever seen, two perfectly uniform rows with each tooth separated an exact hair's breadth from the next. Ordinarily, I'd be slow to let Jen go anywhere with the likes of him, but of course that's not up to me. The one time I did make mention of my concerns, she spelt out the situation so that there could be no misunderstanding. Now, whenever I think of Jeremiah Alsop, the image that fixes in my mind is of that bloated face mangled into the utmost expression of agony, his plump and brilliant fingers cradling his suddenly-traumatised groin area. Jenny has a kick like a leaping cannon. Anyway, she assured me, feeling suddenly and unusually considerate to my feelings, the professor's fondness is for the Asian look, particularly the porcelain perfections of nineteen-year-old Japanese girls. Not so stupid then, your average genius. And he is gifted too, apparently, at weeding out potential groupies from even the most demure of lecture hall situations. No wonder the old boy smiles so much.

'Goodbye, Sean,' Jen says, into my ear, her tone thickened again. She is ebbing back into sleep. 'Call me tonight.'

Our chat ends sooner than I would like, and there are still some things I want to say, want her to say, but I'm not that surprised. She's always been curt. Not really the romantic type, my wife. It does strike me with some disquiet that we can end calls without professing our love for one another, but then we've never been the sort of couple who go in for swooning talk. I think it is her scientific breeding that discourages it, that makes her see such expressions as frivolous. And all the time, through a lot of what little has been said, we seemed to have been sharing the line with somebody busy with the chore of sweeping up a yard of fallen leaves. The constant background rustle has made me feel as though I am part of a game, or of some experiment. That rustling could have been a third party, if a particularly bronchial one. Well, why not? Just because I'm paranoid and all that. Actually, I quite enjoy the notion that I could be some glistening thread in a great dripping web of intrigue, but a large slice of that pleasure comes from knowing that such a possibility would be unlikely in the extreme. The sad truth is that I have nothing of particular interest to hide, no closets full of rattling skeletons. I'm an open book, in that all my indiscretions are already out there, on full show.

After the connection is lost, I continue to talk. Just for a minute or two, so that I can at least feel like I've had the last word. It's a sham, of course, but so what? We all need little lies in our lives, I think, otherwise we wouldn't be even a fraction of the people we want to be.

'So, let me just get this straight in my head, Jen. What you're saying is that there really might be more than one of me out there. Is that it?'

She can't answer, of course, but Christ, that is a mind-blowing thought. The odds are with her, too, the combinations of feature shapes and eye colours are obviously limited. Nothing is infinite, not time, not even space. There are people who scoop lottery jackpots by covering every possible draw. Couldn't it be that I am one of those rare, lucky individuals who find themselves without even looking? I turn my gaze out onto the lobby while the idea sifts through my mind. The day's white light feels as heavy as before, reaching for corners that are, quite honestly, none of its business. Almost by accident, I notice that the mosaic-tiled floor boasts a well-crafted image of a mermaid as its centrepiece. Something dries up inside of me. The bird in my stomach has flown, to be replaced by a closing fist. I shift my body and open my shoulders as much as the narrow confines of the phone-box will allow, but this inner discomfort remains. The mermaid's face is vague but predictably beautiful, her pale hair cascades in wild water-dragged tendrils, and I see that she is well-endowed and just about decent, thanks in the main to a few scales and a couple of well-positioned clamshells. I have always been one of those men who favour a little mystery when it comes to the fairer sex, and the shells are a nice touch, better somehow than having the entire feast on a platter. Some of those Renaissance artists could have learned a lesson from this mosaic, especially the funny ones.

My chest feels as though it is contracting. Maybe I am shrinking. I stare out onto the lobby and feel sure that this is another moment of special significance. Mermaids are full of symbolic meaning. The colours aren't particularly striking, worn pallid, no doubt, from decades of trampling feet, but even so, I can't understand why I haven't noticed her before. Her, the mermaid. For the better part of a week now I have carried myself back and forth through this lobby, a dozen times a day at least, and all that time she has lain there, right under my nose. Maybe waiting for acknowledgement. I realise that I am thinking about naming her, but stop short of that. Wicked things that way lie.

'Goodbye, Jen,' I say, when I have given enough ground to a floor-full of tiles. 'I'll call you later and we can straighten out everything then.' But my voice barely tumbles from my mouth in wisps. On impulse, I add a kissing sound, not at all like me, really, but a small placating gesture that feels right, that feels like it might do a little something towards sating the appetites of the gods or the vibrations that have been devouring my day. Or maybe this kiss is just a last, probably futile, attempt to make myself feel like less of an asshole than I almost certainly am for waking up my wife at five in the morning with a situation that is mine alone. I need two stabs at replacing the receiver on its hook. Then, more out of habit than hope, I rattle the change slot, but find it empty, as always. In all my years of checking, I have never lucked out with so much as a single coin. It is just something that I do. Some people take their hands out of their pockets to cross the road, some people always dress from right side to left. Getting out of the phone-box isn't easy, because I am all turned around.

We tend to think of revelations as great Godly gestures, something to do with burning bushes or parting seas, and almost always with the face of Charlton Heston somewhere in the immediate vicinity. I try showering, but I can't escape the sense that twice in one day, twice in little over one hour, actually, I have suffered revelations that are no less worthy than one of Cecil B. DeMille's patented Technicolor visions. Mine may have lacked a little panoramic scale, they didn't boast any particularly propaganda-rich catchphrases, and I don't expect that people will queue around the block to watch them play out on some multiplex's biggest screen, but to me they are atom bombs, hot and truthful enough to fuse bone to stone. Twenty minutes after retreating to my room I am back in the lobby again. The elevators in these New York hotels seem turbo charged. They leave me tasting a backwash of lunch, even through the fumes of toothpaste. I step through the elevator doors and pause, to take full stock. The white light has dimmed; outside, the rain has finally begun to fall. Through the far revolving doors I can see the street, grey and busy.

This whole lobby area feels full of answers. I glance around, hoping or perhaps dreading that something might just trigger the right questions in my mind, but logging the details isn't as easy as it seems. My thoughts scatter in too many directions, and apart from a couple of vaguely impressionable paintings on the walnut-panelled walls, and a sort-of-pretty-looking desk clerk who stands tapping at the keyboard of a computer and relentlessly tossing her short, bobbed, jet-black hair, there is no further imparting of secrets.

Thinking has given me a thirst. It is not terrible, not yet, anyway, but I know about the twists and turns of slow build-ups. Some people have all the willpower in the world; it seems obvious that someone else must have snagged my share of those goods. The traditional Chinese theory of yin and yang makes natural sense to me; at least, I can appreciate its appeal. Balance is such a lovely notion, even when I happen to find myself on the falling end. Anyway, the point is that when I am thirsty, I drink. The hotel bar lies just to the left of the concierge's desk. Even from the vicinity of the elevator, I can see the curve of the counter through a murky burgundy-draped doorway, and a white-shirted young student-type bobs and weaves in and out of view, busy with the nothing chores of dealing beer-mats and decking the mostly empty tables with little bowls of pretzels and trail-mix. The bar offers an enticing gloom, a place to sit for a few hours and swallow a lot of thoughts, and I am on the verge of surrendering myself to those lazy, wicked charms when my ears pick up the bristles of a stereophonic jazz horn. I once suffered badly at the hands of an obsessive – Elizabeth, my previous – and now I have a severe aversion to jazz. Honestly, I'm talking genuine allergic reaction. It hardly matters, as far as I can see, whether my pain is physically or mentally induced; all I know is that it is real. When I think of all the nights that I spent listening and pretending, maybe even trying, to enjoy that shapeless pap while she sat curled up beside me on the couch, her head twisted to one side, her eyes rolled back into her head and her snake's tongue clacking some incomprehensible time to a gibberish chunk of bebop or a wailing snatch of Herbie Hancock funk, I think that I really must have been head over heels. Stupid in love. So when I hear the first peels of horn, the natural reaction is for my flesh to hackle. Every dribble of blood in my veins wants to run for the hills, and yet, out of some inexplicably masochistic perversion, I march myself across the mermaid and closer to the doorway. My way of fish-hooking my own eyes, I suppose, or flaying my body raw. I get to within perhaps ten feet of the bar when a bass-line walks by, some ugly, hunchbacked Mingus-inspired atrocity that makes me feel sick as a punch in the throat, though even I, jazz bigot that I am, must admit that the drum work is nice, even inspired. Gentle background brush-playing, soothing rather than aggressive, just going on, the sort of fit percussive sound that might be found on a Tony Bennett album. But the horn wears me down, blowing something vaguely familiar. I can't quite place whose lips are puckered with the effort, so it can't be one of the bigger boys. Then the bartender looms into view again, a definite student-type, all right, and he notices me standing in the doorway and smiles. I just make a face, flap my hand at nothing and mutter something about a rain-check. Then I beat the quickest walking-paced retreat that I can possibly manage. The mosaic tiles prove an impressively good conductor, though, and the Mingus-mimic chases me all the way to the revolving doors. I'm sure, in my hasty efforts at escape, that I catch the mermaid smiling, and even worse, the smile feels familiar. But then, isn't that what mermaids are supposed to do, lure unsuspecting victims onto the rocks, in from the open sea to where disaster lies waiting? I tell myself that the smile is nothing more than the simple power of suggestion and I charge outside.

It takes all the effort in the city to hold me from running wild. I lurch like a determined suicide from the precipice of the sidewalk and into the street, lucky I suppose to find myself on a crossing, and let myself be swept along in the fluster of passers-by, my tiny birdsong voice smothered to nothing beneath the commotion of a rushing hour. When the rhythm reveals itself to me I settle for a fast, aimless walk, just drifting, seeking escape, and within ten minutes I am standing on the corner of 42nd and Broadway with my shirt soaked through from both inside and out. The rain matches my mind, at first beating a deluge that clogs the streets and mutilates the drifting crowds, then giving way to a soft fuzz that hardly feels like rain at all, but which, for all its soothing pretence, continues to mercilessly drench. Probably a typical summer's day in New York, I decide, apart from the rain. The sky is a strict snow-cap of unbroken cloud, but the city continues to reach for that, poking and prodding, determined to penetrate. Those towering spires have ambitions of heaven, I suppose. I have a thirst to beat the band now, and my skin prickles with the sweat of my exertions. The first bar I find is dank and foul-smelling, but their sound system is playing early 'seventies Rolling Stones and to my tormented ears Keith Richards' guitar sounds like a dirty, alluring hurricane noise. I order two beers to start with, swallow one in record time while the riffs torch Jagger's sleazy hooting, and rent a seat at the end of the bar, a long way in where the gloom is unremitting and the smoke of illegal things bring dreams and nightmares right to the dusty edge.

'I'll bet that hit the spot,' the bartender says. He is muscle-bound and completely bald, with a wide face that seems to mock his yellow thumbprint of a moustache. When he opens his mouth to speak, I catch the flash of at least one gold crown, and I try not to stare at the tattoos that mar his huge arms and wrists, cheap homely Indian ink stains that meld one into the other, like plants overgrown, running vines. Greens that are nearly blue and reds faded to pink, painting daggers and snakes and bulging women lying vague and shameful beneath wiry yellow spools of hair.

I nod that it does, all right, nod again when he takes my empties and replaces them. 'Efficient,' I mumble, almost to myself, and he considers that for a moment, possibly wondering if he should take offence, then he smiles again and busies himself at the door-end of the bar. The weight of my day falls away, and I sit there, my shirtsleeves growing tacky from the counter, and try to relax. Sweat traces a slow drag from the hairline of my neck down inside my collar, and I flex my shoulder blades to create a sort of canyon. The runnels coax and chase, racking me with shivers. It is a little after three o'clock in the afternoon, and the only other customer, an elderly black man, is asleep in the far corner.

After I have sucked down my sixth beer I raise a hand and suggest that it might be better if I make the switch to wine. Red, I guess. Six beers sounds worse than it really is, because they are only bottles and some brand of gassy American lager at that. I could probably drink these all night long without the slightest ill-effect, but even so, wine does feel like the better option. I know my own system.

The bartender nods and stoops to fumble under the counter, and he makes a decent guess at the limits of my price range. A place like this, they are probably not used to catering for connoisseurs. He does something apologetic with his mouth as he pours the glass, and I understand why even before I take my first sip. Still, I've put away worse in my time, so I grin and bear it.

'Trying to stay sober, huh?' He uses a stained bar towel to polish a convenient beer glass, and it is clear that he is not expecting very much in the way of an answer. I'm not surprised that he seems to understand; bars get filled with a lot of one-way conversations, and spending long days caged behind this counter a man must get to watch a great many acts being played out.

I clear my throat of the bitter wine taste. 'I need to phone my wife later.'

He thinks about that, still polishing the glass in his big hands, and nods. 'I once came across a chunk of advice that steered me well. See if it might fit your situation, or just plain ignore it, if you want. Get some eggs inside you, softer the better. If you know what I mean. Been my experience that they'll fix things one way or the other. You know, bring matters to a head.'

The tattoos seem alive on his arms. 'You ever wrestle?' I ask, for something more to say.

'Wrestle?' He looks at me for a long moment, shows me that gold tooth again. 'I've done my share, I reckon. Never in no ring, though.'

On the sound system, the Stones have given way to Springsteen, the way everything does, eventually. I drink a second glass of wine and pat the counter, trying to make a rumba out of 'Independence Day' and whisper-singing 'Cha, Cha, Cha-cha-cha' instead of the real words. Springsteen sounds as if he is offended by my efforts. 'This wine is terrible,' I say, after the song has finished, and I hold out the glass for more. 'I'll be glad when I've had enough.' Something with a big snare drum kicks from the speakers, and the Boss has discovered Rock 'n' Roll again.

The alarm-clock wakes me hard from a kind of nightmare, one of those dreams that feels not just real but important. A little past four a.m. and a siren is going off, vicious pulsing as incessant as any spinning drill. I sit up and gulp small, risky swallows of air. My tongue has turned to sawdust in my mouth, and the eggs feel like the world's biggest mistake. I try to calculate the time in Tokyo but I've never been much good at figuring out things like time zones. It's not that I can't do it, because the complications are hardly worth talking about, really, just a simple matter of arithmetic, but my problem – I suppose it is fair enough to say one of my many problems – is patience. Even at four in the morning, with not a lot else going on. As soon as my mind starts to ache with the effort, I stop, brace myself and roll from the bed. The aggression of my movement is too much, though, and there is a moment when the darkness deepens and I feel that stifling sweep of blood rushing through me, but just when I am sure that I'll pass out, the air relaxes again. I make it to the bathroom, urinate slowly with one hand bracing my weary body against the cold tiles of the wall, and then I wash my face. The water isn't much, but it helps a little.

To make a call from the room phone costs twice the price of using the telephone in the lobby, and that can amount to quite a bill when the call has to go all the way to Japan. But what convinces me to pay the extra is the thought of falling sixteen floors in a second and a half, penned into that faux-mahogany panelled coffin of an elevator. My stomach can barely manage air just now; the lift would be a torture too far. With what I would be capable of doing, they'd probably never get the smell completely out. I find the piece of paper with the number, safe and sound in the breast pocket of yesterday's shirt, then pick up the receiver and spend a few minutes trying to punch in the several hundred digits required to weave a beeline through the mess of Japanese area codes. For a long time there is nothing but the heavy sigh of the line, but I don't panic, because it is always this way. And eventually, the ringing sound does come, a little click and then the tinny bell sound that once heard can never really leave your head. I resist the urge to count the rings, resist even trying to think of what I am going to say when Jen finally picks up. Knowing my luck she'll be in the shower or something, and I will be bothering her yet again. But I am too tired, really, to care. And too upset; my dream nags at me, the strands of it that have refused to be blown away by consciousness fluttering their tangled tails in the very periphery of my vision. When I close my eyes, awful leftover images explode in my mind, so I can't even enjoy the succour of a moment's rest.

There is no answer. At first, I can't quite accept that, but after a while my arm grows tired of holding the receiver, so I give up. She's probably still at the college, or out to dinner. If afternoon here was the middle of the night there then this ungodly hour know must be, well, some time during the Japanese day. None of that bears thinking too deeply about. I replace the receiver, wondering if I will be charged for the effort if not for the call, and trying not to wonder if Alsop might be in a room somewhere right now, smiling his baby-teeth smile at my wife.

'All right,' I say, in a voice that is hushed out of consideration for the hour but is still audible. 'Let's take a look at this dream, then.' Talking to myself is the sort of habit that only feels odd to me whenever there is somebody there to overhear my words. Jen says that it is a matter of ego rather than insanity, that I simply enjoy the sound of my own voice, but there are times when I catch her looking at me in a funny way, her little nose wrinkled up in irritated folds, and I know that she is wondering if I am doing it just to annoy her. There are some things that should never be said aloud, and a lot of what goes around in my brain, my own particular pearls of wisdom that lie gleaming among the grit of greater general babble, is more often than not unrepeatable.

Naked except for a pair of boxer shorts, I throw myself down on the bed and indulge myself in a groan of pain. Movement has become my enemy, but there is frustration in holding still. Guilt has always been an integral part of my hangovers, even back when I was single and there was no one to harass me for reckless behaviour. Just my way, probably

inextricably linked with a religious upbringing. As a child
I believed in everything: Jesus, witches, ghosts, aliens, the
Loch Ness Monster. I never doubted that the world was
full of magic, demons, miracles and happiness, and growing
up really hasn't done an awful lot to narrow my open mind.
Guilt has always been a precious commodity, something to
be feared and yet treasured. Jenny, who believes in nothing
at all but compound chemical numbers and the formulae
of the universe, has done her best to knock sense into me,
and we've reached a sort of compromise; I let her believe
she's been successful, and she accepts that I'm a lost cause
to logic. It has always been my experience that there is
really nothing quite like a spot of self-flagellation to ease
the worst of a hangover's burden. 'Right,' I say again, 'the
dream.' The words hurt, almost as much as the images that
come charging into my head, trampling out a joyful dance-
step at regaining their rightful place.

I close my eyes and at first there is only darkness and the
pounding of my hangover, but then, gradually, the pieces
of my nightmare pile together and fall back into place. I
see, or feel, that I am myself, but the other me, the one in
the street with the well-groomed moustache and the fine
grey pinstriped suit. I find myself in a plush living room,
some palatial place with chandeliers and tumbling water
features, and am sitting comfortably slumped on a settee
that is all cream-coloured leather, hand-carved oak and
scrolled armrests. The very height of style. On the floor at
my feet, my mermaid lies sprawled and smiling, propped
up on her elbows. Her bedraggled hair gleams the yellow of
sunsets and fool's gold, her flesh has the washed-out, ever

so slightly translucent cleanliness of skimmed milk, and the clamshells cling tenuously in place as a vague and demure gesture against her heaving breasts. There is rock music churning out, the Stones again and then Creedence, and my mermaid flaps her tail happily to the beat and sways her shoulders in a most alluring way. I feel content, as if I have finally made it home after a very long and arduous day. When I reach out, my mermaid takes my hand. Her touch jolts me with life and lust, the pruned skin of her fingertips icy cold. I seem to know and accept that she is Elisabeth, but somehow the Elisabeth that I had always wanted, back when we were together, my vaunted rendition of her that would happily have dragged away and buried all her faults so that what remained behind was perfect. I keep my eyes closed, trying to preserve this vision for as long as I possibly can, but as soon as I begin to think it starts to fray. The fine details are the first to go, the oily rainbow-flecks of her scaly tail, the absolutely perfect smoothness of her shoulder when cupped by my palm, the expensive watch on my wrist and the silken feel of monogrammed socks on my feet, and as I claw in desperation to hold them just a moment longer the entire fantasy unravels hard and fast. Not understanding at all what could qualify this dream in any possible way as a nightmare, I sit up in the bed to find that a few hours have somehow gone, that it is already morning, half-past six. I really feel as if I am a stranger in my own body. Ridiculous, of course, but it is how I feel, awed as I am by the idea of where I have just been.

My hangover has eased a little, though it is nowhere near gone. Dawn has well and truly broken across Manhattan, yesterday's white light replaced by sharp lemon daggers of sunshine that jab through the latticed window to spill in shreds across the floor and onto one low corner of the bed. I know what sort of face waits in the bathroom mirror, that early-thirties face, wind-burnt along the cheeks, creased around the eyes from too long spent outdoors, made old from wind, sun and rain, and too long smelling, and smelling of, the earth. I will be bearded again, my rough-and-tumble mask, the curly black tufts corkscrewing out of my face, granting me a full, wise, harried look that I don't quite deserve. The spools of white will still stain my chin, not even grey but wiry white, random in their placing but favouring one side, my left, turning things a little too askew, prying me just enough out of synch to disturb the general order of things. That is my face, I have lived with it and put up with it through a lot of situations. So why, now, should there be a glimmer of doubt?

I try to tell myself to relax, that the dream is just a side effect of yesterday's adventures coupled with too much beer. With me, even a bottle can be too much. At home, at least I can drink pints, and stout has some weight to it, a particular bulk that can never get too flighty. But here, everything has to be bottles, and fizzy beer has long been an enemy of mine, every bubble a potential nightmare. Yesterday's clothes lie scrawled across the floor, discarded at a run, and coins that have spilled from the pockets glitter like flares, those that catch the sun face on. When the cobwebs threaten to gather again I force myself into action, leaping from the bed and stepping into the shower to try blasting myself back to life. My temples throb with the pulse of some life-or-death chase, and the water chugs and coughs through pipes somewhere deep in the wall, then pummels me with violent, freezing spurts, and I hunch my body in small defence and scream as my suffering finds an entirely new edge. My immediate impulse is to leap away, but I have always been a stubborn old mule where my own pain and repressions are concerned, so I bear the brunt of the spray for as long as I possibly can, taking my punishment, accepting my medicine, and in some small sick way secretly glad of this agony. Then I spent ten minutes or so curled up on the bathroom floor weeping with relief into half a dozen fluffy white hotel towels.

The dream has gathered and decoded my visions. I can feel its weight against me, an insistent, determined pressing. Using New York, with its teeming streets and bedecked lobbies, as His weapon of choice, God – or whoever it is that gazes down on me and pulls my strings – seems to have taken pity on me and offered me a glimpse of the life I might have lived. In many ways a mirror image of my own life, this alternate existence is full of style and affluence, and has me, or some element of me, partnered with a companion who smiles and frolics at my feet and swims in my direction, who flops and flaps to my will and who hums along to the tunes I call. It appears to be a life in which I can sit back and relax, bask in a sense of calm that I hardly recognise because I have never even come close to knowing. The fact that my mermaid is Elisabeth instead of Jenny seems significant too, especially since the truth of the matter is that Elisabeth's manner and nature was never close to serene or pandering, at least not when we were together.

Maybe something would have changed, maybe I needed to get wealthy or grow myself a handlebar moustache. Maybe I needed to take her fishing, once in a while.

I hardly ever speak about our time together; in fact, it is a subject only ever broached now when Jen finds herself in a particularly nasty mood and is tweaking for a row. She'll start pushing and I'll hold out for as long as I can, and then I'll crumble like a cookie in a fist. I've always been tender where pain is concerned. It has been eight years and counting since Elisabeth sent me spinning off out into the big bad world, but even though I managed to find my feet before they were swept out from under me again, the wound of that rejection is still raw. I wonder sometimes if I am just unlucky, if I might have caught some sort of infection of the heart. But I can swear the two eyes out of my head that the old saying about time being a great healer is one almighty suitcase full of shit. Eight years and counting can attest to that hard-earned deduction. I could mention the exact length of time, down to the months and the days too, but that would make me sound pathetic, and I hate sounding that way, even if it is sometimes true. I pick myself up from the bathroom floor, return to my room and begin to dress, very slowly. Running away from dreams, just dismissing them as the ravings of an overactive mind, is all well and good, but what if, sometimes, they are sufficiently forceful that their essence filters through into reality? I vaguely recall reading something along those lines, some book about Native American shamans, I think. And who knows, maybe there is some grain of sense in that. I don't know a great deal about the workings of spiritual things, but then I don't know how airplanes fly, either. Science is as big a mystery to me as God, and some of those white-haired suggestions can be even more difficult to accept. Elisabeth hovers all around me, but as a smiling face framed in long tangles of yellow hair, not at all as I remember her. I can't help but wonder if I have taken a wrong turn, deviated from the path that had been carefully laid out for me.

It is almost seven, and I am more than a little surprised to find that I have worked up an appetite. Waffles, I think, with blueberries, strawberries and maple syrup. Bacon on the side, and lashings of strong hot coffee. The scrap of paper with the telephone number is lying on my pillow, a little rumpled. I pick it up and smooth its creases, then on impulse dial the number again. I'm not expecting much, not thinking about what I'm doing, even. But the line opens midway through the second ring.

'Sean?'

'Hi, Jen.'

She laughs. Actual laughter, a sound that has always made everything seem a little better. It has the same effect now. 'Eight o'clock,' she says.

'What?'

'I told you to call at eight, and here you are, right on time.'

'I'm not disturbing you, am I? I mean, you're not sleeping or showering or anything?'

More laughter, as if I have just said something clever instead of stupid. I listen to her cool breathing, not really sure what to say. 'I'm sorry about last night,' I mumble, 'if it was last night.'

'Are you still worried about that business with your double? Because I'm sorry, Sean. I was half asleep when you called and not thinking straight. What I told you was wrong. There's no one like you in the whole world. You need to remember that. And remember that anyone who might look even vaguely like you is really just a pale imitation. You are the real thing.'

I'm not sure if she is making good-natured fun of me or if she is really trying to be affectionate, but I am surprised by the realisation that it makes no difference either way.

'No,' I tell her, truthfully. 'I'm not bothered by that anymore. I was for a while but I think I've worked it out.'

We talked for a while about small things, how we were getting along in our respective corners of the world, and as usual let the bigger concerns take care of themselves. While I was dreaming, it seems that she has been having a particularly good day, enjoying a successful morning lecture and, later, a nice early dinner with some of her colleagues on the Hokkaido University faculty. The venerable Professor Alsop was, most unfortunately, unable to join them, having come down with an ugly case of food poisoning. 'Bad sushi,' she explains, and goes into detail about the seaweed reacting to the fish. I help myself to the tastier morsels and let the rest drift by. Hokkaido's pretty girls can unlock their doors again, at least until the medication works its magic. When Jen asks about my work I tell her that things are going well, on the whole, that the loose ends seem to be tying themselves up without any great difficulties. Touch wood. I have the thought that marriage should come equipped with an easy-to-use pocket-sized handbook. There are certain pat phrases that can always be relied upon when answering a spouse's casual questions.

Finally, the time comes to hang up. We agree that I should try to call again at around the same time tomorrow. She'll have put away another day, and I'll be waking up to mine. I almost add something affectionate to my goodbye, but words of love take a lot of practice in order to make them sound casual, and I don't want to compromise the aftertaste of a nice conversation, so I hold back. The phone-line clicks shut and I replace the receiver in its cradle. I can picture her in my mind, alone in her room with the television on for company, but with the sound turned all the way down, maybe shucking from her sweater and kicking off her shoes so that she can stretch out on the bed for a little while. She's tired, of course; I know from her time at home that university days can be interminable. Maybe she'll read for a while, but nothing too taxing. She has an odd penchant for old westerns, Louis L'Amour and Zane Grey, that sort of thing. Not the most feminine of subject matter, but each to their own, I suppose. There's nothing like a good plot, she says. And meanwhile, here on the other side of the globe, my own day is just about to begin. I stand by the window for a moment as I slip on my suit jacket. The street below is already busy, the clamour of people and the lines of yellow taxi cabs traipsing their way along east to west, west to east. There seems something tidal about it all.

I step out of the elevator into a lobby that feels surprisingly quiet. The sharpness of the light makes everything feel different, the sun this hotel's most welcome guest. My gaze is drawn, inevitably, to the mermaid, and wisps of the dream rise again in my mind. This time though, maybe because of the sunshine or maybe because of the conversation I've just had with Jenny, I see something that I had somehow missed before. Not all revelations come armed with bolts of lightning. In my dream I am smiling, relaxed in my fine suit and on my expensive settee. My mermaid, Elisabeth, is smiling too, and it really is a picture-perfect scene, very nearly idyllic. I suppose what I am seeing is a state of contentment, yet it does seem strained, not quite natural. I realise that my other self, and the life I might have lived, looks sugar-coated but tastes ever so slightly bitter. Well groomed, basking in the glow of a life that meets my every expectation, I feel a little like I imagine a king must feel. But even kings need to fill their voids, and sometimes happiness just isn't enough. That existence is what it is, dreamlike, and dreams make up only a small corner of our lives. We need them, but we need more than them.

With Jen I have found contentment, stumbled over it without even realising, and I understand, possibly for the very first time in my life, that this is something of true worth. Other words are far more descriptive, like 'love' and 'happiness', but I believe that they are also generally ill-used. 'Contentment' has a far greater resonance. I know that my world is a long, long way down the ladder from anyone's idea of perfect. Our home is nice enough but nothing to write novels about, and we have enough money to get by, more than enough really, though we're not rich by any stretch of even the most febrile of imaginations. The truth is that we're doing okay. Jen can be a real cat sometimes, but there are times when her nice side shines through and those moments are almost worth the price of admission. Artists will wait a long time just to capture the perfect sunset, because good things can be fleeting, but they go quite a distance towards outweighing the negatives. Well-trimmed moustaches, fine suits of clothes and beautiful mermaid wives might seem like dreams come true, but those things are high maintenance. Mermaids won't remain pretty for very long if they lie around all day, sunbathing with the fish. Beards save a lot of time and trouble, you really can't beat a pair of old jeans for comfort, and the pleasures of the making up is very nearly worth the cost of all the infernal bickering. It's only right that Jen is the way she is, one day biting chunks out my cowering carcass, the next devouring me with kisses. That yin and yang business is everywhere, keeping the balance. Happiness, the truly delirious sort, remains the goal for almost everyone, but there is a high price to pay for that. The better option, I think, might be to expend our energies in trying to avoid the other extreme. Contentment lies sprawled across that middle ground and, when we get right down to it, that in-between stretch is really not such a bad place in which to dwell.

ACKNOWLEDGEMENTS

'Heavy Seas' first appeared in the *Evening Echo*, on 10 May 2008.

'The Inner Light' first appeared in the *Evening Echo*, on 30 August 2008.

'A World of Dark-Haired Beauties' first appeared in *Audience* Vol. 3, No. 2, September 2008.

'The Black And Tan' first appeared in the *Cork Holly Bough*, Christmas 2008.

'The Christmas Letter' first appeared in the *Evening Echo*, on 6 December 2008.

'This Bird Has Flown' first appeared in *Read This!* Winter 2008.

'On The Beach' first appeared in the *Hayden's Ferry Review*, Fall/Winter 2008.

'Syzygy' received an Honourable Mention in the 2008 Glimmer Train Open Fiction Contest, and first appeared in *Cezanne's Carrot*, Spring Equinox 2009, winning the Editor's Choice Award.

An early version of 'Secrets' – then entitled, 'A Fine Romance' – first appeared in *Underground Voices*, February 2009.

'Billy O'Callaghan's writing evokes a sense of longing for place and the familiar … His characters are rendered with a lyrical stoicism that lends dignity to all our struggles.'

Suzanne McConnell – *Bellevue Literary Review*

'Billy's short stories are always a pleasure to read …'

John Dolan – *Evening Echo*

In Exile is an eclectic collection of short stories from one of Ireland's brightest literary talents. A marriage is arranged, shotgun style; a terrorist is called upon for one last horrific job; a soldier recalls the trauma of his first kill; an artist, out of pity and loneliness, befriends a hunchback. And in the title story, a man who has built a comfortable life for himself is given a stark reminder of his past, the things from which he has been saved and what he has lost.

These poignant stories give a rare and evocative glimpse into the days and nights of lost people – the weary and the vulnerable. Those whose lives have been wrenched apart, either by the inexorable tilt towards progress, or by the ghosts and shackles of a bygone era.

Billy O'Callaghan has won the 2005 George A. Birmingham Short Story Award, the 2006 Lunch Hour Stories Prize and the 2007 Molly Keane Creative Writing Award. His short stories have been shortlisted for a number of awards, including the 2003 Seán Ó Faoláin Short Story Award, the 2004 RTÉ Radio 1 Francis MacManus Short Story Award, the 2005 Pencil Short Story Prize and the 2006 Faulkner/Wisdom Award.

In Exile

Billy O'Callaghan